The Sound of

Sorrow

A.Niro

"*People to whom sin is just a matter of words, to them salvation is just words too.*"

William Faulkner, As I lay dying

Foreword

The meaning of life...Passion.

I've always had a longing for intelligent and meaningful conversation. The human mind fascinates me profusely. I enjoy *really* getting to know someone, not in a nosey sense, but simply to establish a much deeper understanding and appreciation of how that person came to be who they are known as today.

 In my thirty years on the earth, nothing has catapulted my hopes and fears in to touch quite as much as these last few years and now I can safely say I truly appreciate life for what it is.

Life is a beautiful, ever-changing and wondrous learning curve that will knock you on your ass and sweep you off your feet all in the same breath. Just as you think you know everything, the rug will be pulled from beneath you and you will come crashing down. When you're feeling like you've lost all hope and are struggling to find your way out of the darkness, a warm light will pierce the veil and cast away any feelings of doubt you once harbored.

That's why I find myself so passionate about art and music. The ability to express one's self in another format beyond words is a true talent. Therein lies that sheerness of expression and a coping mechanism for trying to make sense of a bombardment of emotions that our mind can often become consumed with.

The ability to freely express what many others will relate to or simply not understand is liberating. There is no right or wrong when it comes to art. It's simply one person's perspective about a particular subject or feeling being transformed in to an accessible outlet for others to enjoy and interpret as they see fit.

I hope this novel brings you awareness and enlightens you to see things from another perspective.

x A

Chapter 1

LUCY

I ran down the street as fast as my lethargic legs would take me. I mentally scolded myself for being so unfit but quickly shunted the notion to the back of my mind as I approached the downstairs flat entrance. I pounded each and every key on the metallic buzzer begging for someone to give me access via the ground floor when the door in front swung open.

"Can I hel-" the woman tried to speak but I shoved past her and in to the building.

Ignoring the yells and profanities that flew from her mouth, I made my way speedily up the two flights of stairs before reaching his door. My heart had never beaten so fast in its entire life. My hands were trembling and my forehead was clammy with fear.

"Please be ok, please be ok," my mind screamed.

With a shaky hand, I turned the handle seeing it was indeed unlocked before racing inside.

"Dylan!" I yelled.

The lack of response made my skin go cold.
 Dylan's apartment wasn't very big in the slightest so it took me only a matter of seconds to find him.

I gasped, my eyes catching sight of the heap in the centre of the sitting room floor.

My stomach twisted.

I rushed towards him, stark realisation making adrenaline course through my veins. My eyes were roaming over the scene in front of me as my trembling hands went to work of their own accord.

They slackened the belt buckle that was tightly secured around his neck.

My eyes then instantly began scanning their way upwards, catching sight of the ceiling fan. A sliver of leather remained dangling from the fixture.

"Oh Jesus Dylan, what have you done?!" My voice broke before tears began cascading down my cheeks.

With that, the seemingly lifeless body in front of me began to move as Dylan coughed and spluttered beneath me.

I yelped with both shock and utter relief that he was indeed alive.

"Dylan!" I screamed as his eyes flew open.

He quickly shuffled his way backwards, grappling along the floor with his hands. He positioned himself up right, leaning against the wall for support, trying to gather his bearings. All the while his coughing and wheezing continued.

His eyes bore in to mine and I could see the moment he realised that his plan had failed. A desperate sadness washed over him and my heart broke.

In a complete and utter moment of pure and raw desperation, I lunged toward him, my lips smacking straight in to his. He shoved me back, instinctively as his reflexes adapted to what was happening. His eyes grew wide, pleading with me not to do this. He was weak and vulnerable and somewhere in my head I knew this was probably not the right moment to do this but I couldn't contain myself.

He needed to know what he meant to me and I needed to show him. He needed to know that he was important, valued and loved. I leaned back from him momentarily to look at him, *really* look at him.

I was silently pleading with him then, begging for an explanation to what I'd stumbled upon. I also needed to convince him that his life was worth living, that what had happened was obviously a big mistake.

He stared back at me, his eyes reeling with a ton of emotion. Sadness and defeat mixed with lust and longing. There was something else lingering there that I couldn't quite put my finger on. A silent understanding, between friends perhaps? Best friends, to be precise.

I crashed into him once more. This time, my lips were met with his as he kissed me back just as ferociously as I had sought him.

I clambered in to his lap as my hands rummaged through his hair. My mouth moving in sweet succession with his as our tongues began exploring each other's mouths'. My fingers began gently massaging the back of his neck as he groaned. His hands were holding the sides of my face with a vice grip that would have been almost painful if it hadn't felt so good. I'd only ever dreamed of having him kissing me this way and so my mind rejoiced.

The intensity of it all was wreaking havoc with my head and my heart. I was lost in the moment. Overcome with crippling pain and anger at Dylan's attempt to kill himself yet awash with relief and joy at the failed suicide. The possibility of losing him forever awoke something deep in me that I had clearly been harbouring for the better part of a decade. All of those feelings that had been tangled up inside of me were suddenly freeing themselves all the while I continued to bask in Dylan's touch.

I knew Dylan had always been troubled. But, I'd never imagined it would have taken him to this extremity. His hands were roaming over what felt like every inch of my body. He caressed, gripped and even pinched me from my neck, to my waist and then settled on my breasts. I arched into him in response as my own moan echoed against the empty walls. I'd never been so needy in my life.

I could have let it continue for what would have felt like hours without interruption until my very weighty conscious suddenly kicked in.

"Dylan, Wait!" I pulled away from his mouth just long enough to grab his attention.

My dark eyes gazed at him deeply as his glistening blue eyes studied me while we both tried to catch our breaths.

"What were you thinking?" I whispered as my hand softly traced the bruising above his collarbone.

He visibly shuddered at my touch before wincing a little as his hands left my body and gently rubbed at the self-inflicted wound he now wore around his throat.

He became motionless again for a little while after that, his eyes also catching a glimpse of the snapped belt fragment visible from above.

He needed help. Reassurance. Distraction. Anything that would take his mind off of the reason as to why he had considered ending it all just moments ago.

He lowered his head as his body began to shake slightly beneath me.

"I'm such a fuck up," he mumbled so quietly under his breath that I almost didn't catch it.

His shaky hands ran through his hair before he gripped it and tugged hard. He let out a pent up roar and then slammed his knuckles in to the floor at either side of his hips.

His frustration caught me by surprise. And then, in a completely unexpected twist, my own anger pulsated through me and made my blood boil.

"What the fuck were you thinking?!" I yelled this time before the palm of my hand made impact with the soft side of his left cheek.

He grimaced, his hand instinctively rising to feel where the red handprint began to show on his face. His eyes bugging out a little as he stared at me, in shock it seemed by my reaction.

My hands flew to my mouth and I gasped.

"Shit, Dylan, I'm sorry!" I mouthed, sudden guilt enveloping me at my actions.

"It's ok, I deserve that," He cried defeated, shaking his head and lowering his eyes.

His humility made my insides ache.

I grabbed his hand from the side of his face and placed it back on the side of my own.

"Look at me, please," I begged.

He raised his head and forced his eyes upon mine.

A thousand different emotions were bubbling beneath the surface of those deep blue eyes but I willed myself not to get caught up in that just yet.

"I need you," I breathed. "Like, really need you," I emphasised.

He shook his head.

"You don't need me," he argued, "No one does. I'm the one that's always needed you. *Nobody* needs me. Besides, you have Reece," he choked out.

My head began to spin.

He needed salvation and fast.

"What about Iris?" My mind shot back instinctively.

He simply scoffed, dismissively.

"What about Trey, and Rory?"

He just sat silent.

It was as if he had forgotten about the people who were supposed to mean the most to him. His eyes gave away his guilt then. He really hadn't thought this through. My stomach twitched in agony again at this unveiling.

I hadn't even spared a single thought for any one of them in the moment either. Not once. Not for one tiny second. Reece was my boyfriend after all, and surely he deserved better than this. And Iris was good for Dylan, or at least that's what I had originally thought. Trey and Rory and the band had been gathering more success recently. Surely that was worth something? Not enough to prevent Dylan from wanting to disappear forever though which upset me profusely.

The mention of the names of all the people closest to us did nothing to quell my sudden lust for Dylan. I could no longer convince myself that what I shared with Reece meant more than what I had with Dylan. I loved Reece of course, just not as much as Dylan. I knew right there I needed Dylan more. He was my first friend. He was my true best friend. He was my comic, my comfort, my courage. He was my strength and my moral compass. He was talented and smart and caring and didn't have a vindictive bone in his body. He'd been there for as long as I could remember. Always. I couldn't picture going through a single special moment in my life if he couldn't be a part of it. My world would end with his. If Dylan was gone, I wouldn't want to remain. He was genuine and compassionate and suddenly, my hands were finding their way back to his face.

"Lucy," he whispered, his panicked eyes trying in desperation to read mine.

"Dylan," I breathed his name as if merely saying it out loud would affirm my feelings for him.

He looked much more present and alert this time, despite everything that had happened moments ago.

"We can't," he started batting my hands away softly as he lowered his head again.

"We *can*," I pleaded, pressing his shoulders into the wall behind him as my weight continued to bear down on his lap.

"I love you Dylan," My voice spoke the words loud and true.

I couldn't fathom why I'd never truly said it to him before now.

His brow furrowed his eyes scanning left and right of my features trying to make sense of this.

"Look Lucy, you found me, you saved me. You got me through my hard times and you've seen me at my worst. I'll never forget that. But the last thing I need right now is your pity or for you to make out with me because you feel sorry for me or something..." he trailed off, clearly misinterpreting my true intentions.

"I don't want to kiss you because I feel sorry for you Dylan," I stared at him. "I want to kiss you because it feels good. Because I love you. Because deep down, I've always loved you. I only wish I'd realised it sooner. We could have been so much more!" I exclaimed.

He shook his head in disbelief, his heart racing against his chest and his groin clearly affected by the close proximity of my body straddled on top of his.

Surely this wasn't entirely one-sided? I remembered the way Dylan had looked at me over my adolescent years. He'd always been a gentleman but I caught him staring at me more often than not without his knowledge. I knew that look. The one he currently had. It was the kind of look reserved for the women he wished to pursue, only deeper than that. This one was only for me. He'd done a stellar job of trying to disguise it over these last few years but I knew it had been there all along.

I ran my hands from his shoulders, down the lengths of his toned arms and entwined our fingers together.

I watched as his eyes roamed over our clasped hands and then found their way back upon my own.

"You're serious?" he stated, desperate sincerity in his tone.

"This feels right, you and me. Like it always has been. Tell me you feel the same?" I suddenly grew wary of how much I was banking on his response.

He nodded his head slowly at first, his heart and mind coming together in a culmination of agreement. His eyes brightened and the tiniest flicker of something closely resembling hope appeared moments later.

"Lucy, I...I don't know what to s-" but I cut him off with another chaste kiss.

'Enough talk,' I thought to myself, my body aching to emerge itself in this new found feeling with Dylan.

This time, he didn't delay in responding. I knew his answer in the way he wrapped his arms securely around me bringing me even closer to him than I thought physically possible.

"This does feels right," he whispered against my neck in-between leaving a trail of hot, wet kisses along my jawline.

"*So* right..." I moaned.

"Fuck, Lucy...you've no idea how long I've wanted to do this," his husky voice made every part of my body sing with need for him.

That need surpassed new heights as I willingly lay my back against the floor. Dylan peered from above me before our bodies began grinding and writhing against one another in a flurry of lust-filled longing. Our kiss deepened and grew much more soft and sensual as he looked down at me. I opened my eyes momentarily in a desperate bid to take in the realism of it all but instead of seeing him, I found myself catching a glimpse of the discarded belt and buckle out of the corner of my eye. It made my stomach wince. Dylan peeled back from me reluctantly, following my line of vision and the cause for my disdain.

I looked up at him, apologetically before watching him grab the inanimate object with his right hand and launch it across the room. The sound of the leather smacking against the wall jolted me.

My heart was in my mouth. How could this same person ever have contemplated that me, or this world would have been any better off without him in it.

"I'm sorry," he breathed hurriedly, his eyes conveying his outrage at himself for what could have been.

"I know," I replied, my voice shaky and my breath ragged.

My hands grabbed hold of his face at either side and pulled him down towards me so we could pick up where we left off.

A deep groan rumbled at the back of Dylan's throat as my hands shifted toward his hips, desperately trying to rid him of his shirt.

"I want this so fucking bad," He cried as he raised his arms and allowed me to pull the shirt over his head.

"Scratch that," His mouth wandered past the clavicle of my neck and trailed towards my lower stomach, my hands trailing down his bare chest and settling on his lower back.

"I want *you* so fucking bad," he corrected and I grinned.

"I want you *too*," I sighed as he raised the hem of my shirt and dipped his tongue in to my belly button.

My hips bucked towards him in response.

His fingers began unbuttoning my blouse before he shed me of the restrictive material. His gaze seemed hauntingly fixated on my face as he unfastened my jean shorts and practically ripped them from my flesh, leaving me exposed in only my bra and knickers. His lips crashed against mines once more, nothing but the thin, black lace of my underwear separating his body from mine. That and his low cut jeans which he soon stripped off.

My eyes trailed over the lines of ink that adorned his toned body and the flex of his muscles as he held himself hoveringly above me, leant on elbows that were either side of my frame. He paused to look at me then and I swear those eyes could see in to my soul.

With burning desire and a desperation that had me practically trembling beneath him with need, his fingers found their way to my already wet slit.

I moaned as he teased the flesh there, rubbing circles around my clit with his thumb and then dipping his index finger gently inside. His eyes bore in to mine watching my every reaction.

My mouth fell open as I groaned and my hands gripped harder in to his defined shoulders. His quickening pace and the insertion of a second finger doing the kind of things to my body that women's dreams are made of.

"Yes," I hissed. "Right there..." I begged as he found my sweet spot.

His upturned fingers inside me were positioned in a sort of 'come here' summoning motion as he stroked the swollen flesh back and forth. My body tensed and relaxed and my pelvis shot up to meet his body with every thrust of those digits.

"You're so fucking wet for me babe, I love it," He grinned before nibbling on my left nipple and earning himself another moan in turn.

"I just have to taste you," he whispered, as he moved his hot mouth down the centre of my chest and towards my groin.

I was already moments away from coming at the thought of his mouth on me and he knew it. My nails scratched against his spine and my breath hitched in my throat as soon as he found me. He sucked and licked on my clit before running his tongue across my folds, burying his beautiful face between my legs.

I propped myself up slightly from the bed so I could get a better look at him. The view was even better than I imagined. The man who had been my best friend for ten years. The man I adored. The man who stood by me, protected me and loved me.

The intensity of having Dylan perform such an act was truly breath-taking.

We were both very much alive and currently caught up in the midst of a powerful and intimate moment.

Things were never ever going to be the same again.

With that thought, I leaned back, my voice calling out his name as I came hard beneath him. Collapsing backwards on the bed, I felt myself falling apart underneath him, like warm butter through hot hands.

Chapter 2

Lazily stretching my arms above my head I let out a big yawn before slowly prising my eyes open. The sunlight was streaming in through a tiny gap in the curtains so I knew it was well past early morning.

Gathering in my surroundings, my mind did a short replay of last night's events.

I quickly rolled over in search of the beds main occupant and found Dylan sitting upright with his back against the head board next to me.

His ruffled hair and drowsy eyes looked adorable from this angle so I smiled, muttering a bashful "Hey," before pushing myself up to match his posture.

"Hey sleepy head," he grinned but I could see the pure exhaustion etched across his face.

My eyes couldn't help but see the angry, purple bruising now adorning all of Dylan's neck and collarbone, just above the tiny tattoo handwritten across his chest that read 'Dana' in italic. Dylan's older sister who was killed by a drunk driver all those years ago.

It had been a long time since we'd spoken about her. I remembered the incident like it was yesterday and recalling the heartache it brought Dylan's family still felt as raw now as it had done back then.

My hand moved of its own free will to trace the line of ink.

"When did you get this?" I asked groggily, my voice still hoarse from lack of sleep and last night's activities.

"A few years back," he admitted.

His hands were clasped in front of him now and he was playing with his fingers nervously like he didn't know what else to say.

I knew Dylan and his sister were close but I don't think I'd ever really appreciated just how much. It seemed that there was a lot I hadn't fully paid attention to over the years. So much history when it came to the man sat next to me. So much heartache and secrets.

"So, are we going to talk about what happened last night," I began, drudging up the dreaded elephant in the room.

"Which part?" Dylan prompted and it kind of threw me off guard.

At least he was willing to face up to it. I half expected him to run for the hills. Then again I should have given him more credit. He'd never run from me before. Why should this be any different.

"All of it I guess..." I tried to think of the best way to start but my head hurt from the barrage of questions and memories colliding in my mind.

"How about the part where you nearly killed yourself last night?" My words were like daggers and I knew it sounded much harsher than my original intent but I needed answers.

Dylan sighed and kept his gaze on his hands.

I leaned over taking his right hand in mine in a show of affection and a plea of patience as he worked up the courage to speak.

"I honestly don't know what came over me," He began.

He sounded as tired as he looked but I could tell he had clearly spent the last few hours mulling over what this conversation was going to be like.

I remained silent, knowing it was just as important for him as it was for me for to hear him confess the motive for his actions.

"I noticed I had a missed call, shortly after we finished playing our set at the club," he spoke.

My mind recalled the text I'd received from Dylan at the beginning of the night reminding me that him and the boys had a gig that night. I'd quickly replied, apologising that I had work and wouldn't make it but offered to catch up with them later. On my break, Reece had also called me to fill me in on how it had gone. He said it had been a really good gig in a thousand capacity venue which was practically sold out. An intimate setting with the home crowd to welcome the boys back from yet another tour. From what I'd heard from Reece, people had been paying close attention to the lads and there had been flocks of girls screaming. The crowd had been fully engaged and there was nothing but good vibes throughout their performance. I remember how animated Reece sounded on the phone which was unusual because he wasn't particularly keen on live music. I also remember feeling a little gutted about missing the show.

I waited for Dylan to continue.

"It was my mother," he explained and I grimaced.

I could almost for-see where this was going.

"We were just about to finish packing up our gear when I noticed Cody smoking a cigarette near the fire exit," my hands went cold.

Dylan's stepfather Cody had been nothing but abusive since his real father left years ago. His mother could not see past his charms and always chose his side over her own son's. Cody was a despicable human being, leaching on the weak and forever getting in to trouble. He'd laid in to Dylan countless times as a teenager yet his mother had done nothing about the violence. It was almost as if she thought he deserved it. Dylan and I had done our best to stay away from them these last few years. Dylan had been so much more at ease with himself since cutting the pair of them out of his life.

Cody however, obviously couldn't keep away forever.

"I didn't want to cause a scene in front of the lads so I thought it best to approach him rather than have him come over to us. So I made my way over to Cody, telling the guys I'd be back in a minute while they continued loading the van," he took a deep breath at this point.

I squeezed his hand reassuringly, knowing this was painfully hard for him to think about.

"I asked him what he was doing here and he gave me some bullshit excuse about my mother needing to see me and some money that I apparently owed her," he tensed.

"Basically, because the band are now becoming more successful, he thinks this is the perfect opportunity for some fucked up family reconciliation so that he can get his hands on whatever cash may be rolling in my way," he spat.

"I'm not going to repeat exactly what he said to me," he inadvertently grimaced at the memory, "but his words struck something in me and it was like a switch suddenly flipped."

I tried to picture the scenario in my mind.

"I told him to 'fuck off', flipping him off but not before he grabbed me by the scruff of my shirt and slammed me against the brick wall. I punched him square in the jaw after that and then next thing I know the boys had ran towards us to break it up."

That's when I noticed the faintest swell across the knuckles of his hand currently laced in mine. He'd gotten in to a fight with his stepfather, no doubt arguing about his mother, just as they always did. Whatever Cody had said to Dylan had obviously triggered a chain of events that ultimately lead to Dylan wanting to take his own life. Rage pulsated throughout me to my very core.

"What happened after that?" I urged, getting closer to the harrowing truth.

"In all honesty, a lot if it is still kind of a blur," he admitted, seemingly frustrated with that fact.

"I went back to the bar inside with Trey and Rory and we started ordering shots. A bunch of girls came up to us to chat about the show and then I remember Iris started giving me a hard time about them," he closed his eyes now in recollection.

"We haven't been getting along much these days. She's always crazy jealous and accusing me of getting up to no good. I'm sick of it," he spat.

"Before long, we ended up in an argument too and I decided I'd had enough. I apologised to the guys before making my way towards the exit. My phone rang again, but this time I decided to answer."

"My mother screamed and yelled at me, blaming me for her new black eye. She said Cody had come over simply to see the band play tonight and that I'd acted out and embarrassed him in front of everyone in the club. She claimed I was an ungrateful bastard and Cody has done nothing but try to help me. Honestly, nobody even fucking saw the scuffle between us except for my band mates, yet my mother was going off on one about how I'd ruined his reputation or some fucking shit." he hissed.

His utter disgust and contempt as he described the conversation with his mum was palpable, yet throughout his retelling of the story I sensed his disappointment in the woman he knew as his mother. It was heartbreakingly sombre.

"I was just about to hang up the phone, having had enough bullshit for one night when something she said cut right through me..." he paused.

I knew this was it. The nail in the coffin. The final push over the edge. The cause that had driven him to come home and wrap his belt around his neck and attempt to suspend himself from the ceiling. I closed my eyes.

"You're nothing but a fuck up," he said, *"It should have been you that died instead of Dana,"* he relayed his mother's words.

My skin ran cold.

How could any mother willingly wish the death of her only son?

I felt like I could vomit at any given second.

We stayed quiet for some time. Dylan unable to describe what he did next and me unable to offer any further words of comfort at his mother's harrowing retort. She had unwittingly sealed his fate and driven him to do the unthinkable. I prayed that she and Cody were one day held accountable for their actions. No child should be made to feel so unloved by parents who were responsible for their wellbeing.

"I was really drunk by this point. And you know, I'd just argued with Iris, and you were at work," I cringed, "I just couldn't see any other way," his voice and those words broke me in two.

A silent tear trailed down my face and I let it.

"I was convinced my mother's words were true. As if still being here in this world was some sort of sick punishment for being alive instead of Dana. Dana deserved to be here more than I ever did. She was the popular one, the smart one and the one who actually made my parents proud. She was the one so full of life and love and knew just how to make everyone feel good and happy. Her death was the reason my parents split and the cause of my mother's addictions and my new stepfather. If I had died instead of her, then none of the bad shit would have happened. My mum and dad would have continued living in their happy little lives with their perfect daughter. I didn't think it would matter if I was simply gone. Not to anyone," he stated, part of him still seemingly believing his words.

I couldn't stay quiet anymore.

"It would have mattered to *me* Dylan. More than you can ever know. You have always been there for me and I would never have gotten through school if it hadn't been for you. You fought for me and defended me like no one else ever has. You protected me and looked out for me and you always had my back. I confided in you, I believed in you and I still do. I owe everything to you Dylan. All the nights you'd sneak over to mine to escape Cody and your mum. You may not have realised this back then but I needed you just as much as you needed me. I can't ever repay you for that. And besides, for all you know your father would have still left your mother. The grief of losing a child, any child, is beyond repair. You're so convinced that life for others would have been better with you gone but you can't know that for sure. You mean something to me Dylan. You always have and you always will. Some days, you mean everything to me," yet again another truth I spoke aloud.

He held my hand a little tighter and I only hoped he would come to realise his worth one day. But it would take time. Like all things.

"How did you know I'd be here, where you found me last night?" He then asked, breaking the quiet once more.

"I bumped in to Iris after my shift at work. Reece texted me telling me to meet everyone back at the club for drinks since I missed the gig. When I got there, Iris came rushing up to me. She told me you two had gotten in to a fight and that she couldn't find you. She mentioned something about over hearing the guys talk about you fighting and I just knew something wasn't adding up. I've known you for over ten years and never once have I known you to argue in public with a girl or be violent without first being provoked," I motioned.

"I can't explain it but suddenly I had this strange feeling in my gut that something was really wrong. I told Reece I needed to find you but he told me to leave you and tried to convince me that you were fine. I refused to accept that and so ran out of the club moments after arriving. I tried looking for you at all our usual hangouts but then I remembered Iris saying that you had wanted to be alone. That's what triggered my worst fear," I explained.

Dylan nodded in seeming understanding.

"It's like that old dog story...dog's generally love companionship, but they seek out solitude when they know they are about to die. Most of them crawl under sheds or hide behind the couch. You've always hated being alone. The countless nights spent sneaking in to my room or crashing at your band mates' houses taught me that. So when Iris said you just went off and wanted to be alone...It's the first thing I thought about," I confessed.

"You've had this apartment for over three years now but yet you hardly ever spend a night in it unless Iris is here with you. Your clothes are still in boxes by the wardrobe and you have no pictures on the walls. You barely have any furniture except for that couch and this bed which I know you barely ever use for sleeping in, so I just knew this was likely the place you would feel most alone,".

My analogy may have been a little bit of a stretch but I also knew that Dylan and I shared a connection like no other. It was apparent to me now that although there were certain things about Dylan he may have kept hidden from others, I still had a pretty good intuition when it came to him.

The air around us had grown colder and the beam of sunlight from earlier on was now hidden behind some darkening clouds.

Goosebumps began to rise on my arms and I involuntarily shivered from the light chill. Dylan automatically swung his arm around me, pulling me closer to him. I breathed in his scent, resting my head on his chest as he scooted down the bed a little to get more comfortable.

"Fuck Lucy, I can't believe how well you know me sometimes," he breathed out and I smiled.

"I feel the same way about you and how well you know me," I replied.

"I'm glad it was you that found me, as horrid as it must have been," he grimaced at the thought.

"Imagine it had been the other way around," I propositioned and his body physically tensed.

"You mean me finding you like that?" His brows furrowed and the fear in his eyes was evident.

I nodded.

"Fuck that, I couldn't live with myself after that," he blurted out.

"Exactly how I felt. So please, Dylan, don't ever put me through that again?" I begged and he relaxed.

"I can't believe we finally had sex!" his words signalling the end of the serious conversation for the time being as a chuckle rattled through his body.

"And in my OWN bed!" He exclaimed.

"I can't believe we had sex either," We both laughed as he ran his fingers expertly through the dark strands of my slightly matted hair.

It was as though nothing between us had changed yet in many ways everything had. I'd grown accustomed to these usual small gestures of affection between us we had shared over the years but there was so much more intimacy in them now. My mind wondered if we'd have been better off as more than friends to begin with.

I sighed contently.

"There's no going back from this now, right?" Dylan spoke as his deftly fingers continued their plight through my tangled curls.

The motion was making my eyes drift and almost lulling me back in to a more peaceful sleep.

"Nope," I breathed, earning another chuckle from him in response.

"So this is…official? We're both in agreement that this is more than just sex right?" Dylan eyed me wearily, making sure that I understood his request.

"It's official. I want us to be more than just friends, and not just friends with benefits either. Part of me wonders why the hell we never tried to make this work years ago?" I answered truthfully, my brain conjuring all sorts of possible missed opportunities between us.

I briefly tried to recall some of the more personal and intimate moments I'd shared with Dylan over the years. There had been times I had longed for something more between us but my cautious mind was quick to remind me that Dylan had an awful reputation with the girls. Our entire school had catalogued him as the go to guy for a one night stand and that didn't bode well with me. I wasn't a prude but I had respect for myself. I also didn't want to change the dynamic between us. Dylan had never pursued me romantically before and that's the side of him I was keen to admire. It proved he had goodness inside him and a heart. He made me feel safe and wanted and sex would have only complicated things between us.

"Yeah, but I'm sort of glad it hasn't happened before," he replied, his hands still working their way over my head.

"Really? How so?"

"Can you imagine if we'd started dating when we'd first met? We were kids. You were much younger than me too. Everyone would have flipped! Besides, I was a fucking mess for a long time. I still am some days. Are you sure you want to get in to that?" Dylan's eyebrow raised speculatively.

I reached up to catch his jaw and pulled him toward me for a tender kiss. He pulled back, cupping the side of my face with his palm awaiting my response.

"That day, at the barbeque, when we first met? You had this devilish smirk in your eyes and a sulky pout at your father for dragging you to such an event. But when I tripped on the concrete slab and grazed my knee, you were the first one to come over and help me up. I was crying and my mum kept trying to get me to stop but the tears kept streaming. Do you remember what you said?" I paused and he smiled.

"I told you that it was not your fault and that the path was stupid," he chimed and we both laughed at how juvenile we were.

"Exactly. I stopped my sniffling and my smile quickly returned because you knew exactly how to cheer me up. You've always known what to do or say to fix me. Even back then. I may have been a little girl but from that moment, I knew I wanted to be close to you".

"And still, after everything we've been through, I can't imagine a future without you, by my side. We'll have each other's backs. For as long as we can. I know we will," I exhaled.

Dylan closed his eyes for a moment and then peered back at me.

"I don't deserve you Lucy, truly," he began and I quickly shushed him with my index finger.

"Nonsense. We deserve each other, we're good for each other. I just know it. I always have," he thumbed the side of my cheek before his lips met mine once more.

I felt my body melt beneath his touch. Each new sensation sending me further into unknown territory with him. There was no going back. I didn't want to go back from this. I needed his fingers caressing my skin, his strong arms around me and the scent of him as I buried my head beneath his chin. It felt like coming home. Like every other attempt at a normal relationship had been futile. Like we were the only two people in the world who were remotely compatible. I was his and he was mine. Finally. The internal elation made my heart sore and my stomach flutter.

Our kiss broke long enough for Dylan to speak.

"I think we should wait a while before we make our situation public though. You know, give it some time, Iris and Reece....They're both going to freak out," he suggested.

"Mmm," Was the only curt reply I could muster. I was far too relaxed to use my voice.

"Or I could continue to see Iris AND you if you'd prefer?" That earned him a playful smack along his ribs.

"Just checking you're still listening," I could hear him smile.

No words can describe how good it felt to hear Dylan joking and playing around like his usual self. The contentment of his arms around me and his gentle caresses as I listened to the sound of his voice soon had me nodding off again. He kissed my forehead before snuggling closer. It felt perfect. Too good to be true.

And then a shrill voice began shrieking his name.

"DYLAN!"

My eyes flew open.

At the foot of the bed stood a girl, dressed in last night's clothing.

It was Iris.

Chapter 3

"What the fuck!?" She began yelling as I scrambled from Dylan's arms.

I pulled the covers up to my chin trying to protect my modesty. Although whatever morsel of dignity I thought I had left was most likely already gone. We'd been caught. We had no chance to explain. The guilt rose in my throat like bile.

"Shit Iris, I can explain," Dylan began, quickly pulling on the boxers he had discarded earlier from the side of the bed.

His face was white with fear.

"Don't fucking come near me you lying bastard!" Iris screamed. "How could you do this to me!?"

I'd never heard her use such vulgar language before. I guess she had a good reason to display said language now. Her hands were balled in to fists at the sides of her tiny waist and her mascara was running down her cheeks with every tear. My stomach was knotting again at the pain we'd bestowed on the girl stood before us. I felt like a complete and utter bitch. Our perfect unification ruined. Hearts were to be broken.

"It's not what it looks like, I swear," Dylan attempted but I saw him visibly cringe at how unconvincing he sounded.

"Oh really!?" Iris roared back sarcastically. "So it's totally normal for the two of you to be lying in bed together, with no FUCKING CLOTHES ON!"

The girl had spunk, I'd give her that. If it had been me I'd have fled the room ages ago. But Iris was tougher than she looked and she stood her ground. I could see she wanted answers I just didn't think she would be able to handle the truth once she heard it out loud.

Dylan stood shirtless between the bed and Iris. I was still frozen in place on the right hand side of the bed, watching this all play out like some terrible soap opera. Only this was real life and there were real feelings at stake. The last thing I wanted was for Dylan to start having doubts. He'd already gone through too much.

Iris started rummaging through her shoulder bag hurriedly in search of something. Dylan cautiously moved towards her, no doubt fearing whatever her next move may be.

"Iris, what are you doing?" He tried to prise an answer from her, stepping even closer to where she stood.

"Move the fuck back Dylan, I swear to god!" She screamed, pointing her mobile phone in his direction.

"Okay, Okay!" Dylan replied, his hands held up in defence.

I was so caught up in the shouting that it took me a moment to realise Iris's eyes were now focused on me, disgust evident in her stare as she pressed her phone against her ear.

"Hello? Yes, Reece, it's Iris," My stomach flipped.

"Oh fuck, oh fuck," I thought to myself, "What the fuck is she doing?"

"Come on up to Dylan's place, please, it's important," She urged, her eyes never leaving mine and a vicious smirk now tweaking at the edge of her mouth.

I wanted to kick her in the head.

"Iris, what the fuck are you doing," Dylan sounded panicked now as he tried to reason with her.

"You're going to get what's coming to you, you lying sack of shit! How could you do this? I thought we had something special?" her words were a mix of pure anger and utter devastation.

"No one cheats on me and gets away with it. You're going to pay for this. Mark my words," She spat, stuffing her phone back in her bag and folding her arms across her chest.

Dylan turned around to face me, the first time he had looked at me since Iris had appeared. His eyes were laced with worry and he had a concern in them that I know he had reserved only for me. In the same breath, his eyes grew hard and he had a strict resolve in them. Dylan wasn't prepared to back down. He was going to fight for me, for us. Just like he'd promised. I felt conflicted. I also knew this was going to end badly so I made a move to grab my clothing that was strewn across the floor when Iris barked again.

"Don't you fucking move! Don't you fucking move you slut! Reece will be here any minute now and he needs to see this! Stay where you are!" She'd reached hysterical mode.

The tone of her voice made me jump out of my skin but I couldn't sit here and do nothing while all of this unfolded.

Defiantly choosing to ignore her words, I found my own voice.

"Iris, listen. You don't have to do this. Please, we never meant to hurt anyone. It's deeper than you think. There's so much to explain," I tried but a loud 'bang' from the room next door drew our attention away.

Jesus that was fast.

He must have been waiting downstairs?

A strange feeling wrapped itself around me and I froze.

With that, Reece barged through the open door and stood by Iris. His flustered and confused face looking from her, to Dylan and then eventually settling on me. Me, who was now only partially covered by the bed quilts in my mid-attempt to retrieve something to wear.

"What the fuck?" Reece's words were pretty much identical in tone to Iris's as she'd first entered the room and I stupidly almost snickered.

My head was a mess and the nerves were obviously making me want to react a little crazily.

"I caught them Reece, I caught the pair of fuckers cheating on us!" Iris practically sing-songed as she moved towards him and placed her hand on his shoulder.

I could see the tension in his biceps from my positon on the bed.

"Reece please, it's not her fault, whatever you've got to do, take it out on me," Dylan spoke and Reece's stance changed.

He flipped Iris's hand from his shoulder in one violent shrug and shoved Dylan against the bed. Reece's hands were wrapped around his throat before I could barely blink and my instinct suddenly took over.

"Reece STOP!" I yelled before launching myself from the side of the bed and toward the two guys who were now slammed against the foot of it. No longer concerned about my nude state.

I punched my fist repeatedly against one of Reece's toned arms until he eventually slackened his grip around Dylan's throat enough to allow him some air. Dylan fell to the ground coughing and grasping at his chest, clearly in extreme pain from the injuries he had inflicted upon himself yesterday and Reece's attack on him just now.

I watched in horror as Dylan got to his feet and Reece quickly sucker-punched him hard in the jaw. Dylan's hand flew to his mouth, dabbing gingerly at the smattering of blood that was now trickling there before regaining an upright position. Reece never retaliated though. He simply stood there, bracing himself for the next hit. It never came.

Reece grabbed me by my shoulders, jerking me around to face him. Tears were threatening in his eyes as he looked at me.

"How could you do this?" He pleaded, his voice near breaking point.

My own tears began to fall freely as I peered up at the man in front of me. The man I'd spent the last few years of my life preparing a future with. Reece was a good guy, great in fact. It just wasn't meant to be. My heart had already been set on someone else's. He'd never stood a chance. I wish I knew how to explain.

"I'm sorry Reece, truly!" I pleaded. "I never meant for this to happen. There's just so much more to the story than you know. I never wanted to hurt you. I just can't lose him. Dylan tried to kill himself last night," My words came rushing out without thought.

I heard Iris gasp from the back of the room and then Reece let go of me.

"What?" He asked incredulously, his eyes giving away a fleet of emotions as he tried to process them at rapid speed.

"It's true," Dylan spoke hoarsely, leaning against the bed, crossing his arms and wrapping them around his bare chest.

"If it weren't for Lucy, I'd be dead. She saved me last night," He whispered.

Reece's face was awash with some emotion I couldn't quite read as his eyes studied the bruising evidently plastered around Dylan's throat and collarbone.

All the while, Iris remained silent.

"I don't understand, " Reece spoke. "None of this makes any sense. I thought you two were just friends?" Reece questioned, his eyes roaming over my naked form.

I cringed, and wrapped my arms around my breasts while leaning forward in a position to shield my most intimate part. I picked up the white oversized shirt from the floor and turned around, carefully pulling the garment over my head. I slipped on my knickers and then my jean shorts. Everyone remained quiet as I did so.

The embarrassment of it all had my cheeks flushed red from the sheer mortification of having to endure so much eyes on me in my most vulnerable state.

I stole a glance at Dylan who was now perched on the end of the bed, his eyes cast down as he tried to get his breath back, his mind clearly foggy and his thoughts his own.

"Let me explain," I ushered, trying to grab a hold of Reece's hand.

I needed to defuse the situation and fast.

"No need. I get it. I knew you guys were more than just friends. I've always known that. I just thought..." He trailed off, his eyes filling as he clinched his fists together in desperation.

"You told me you loved me. And I believed you. But I should have known better," he looked at me then and my heart ached from the pain I'd clearly put him through.

"Reece, I..." I stuttered but it was no use.

The pain in his face was evident. No words would ever soften this devastating blow. We'd made our bed and there was no turning back.

I tried once more to reach him, my hand seeking out his, but he shrugged it away. Just as he had Iris's earlier.

With one last glance through those glazed eyes, I watched as Reece turned around, making his way towards the door.

He left the room in silence and vacated the apartment the same way he had come in. Iris looked from me to Dylan, obviously disappointed with the turn of events and then followed suit. Her departure was signalled with the slamming of the front door.

Snapping myself back in to the moment, I wiped at the stray tears still streaming down my cheeks. I went and sat next to Dylan on the end of the bed. I placed my hand softly on his thigh as his hand wrapped itself around my own.

I gentle rubbed at the trickle of blood at the edge of his mouth with the pad of my thumb.

"Are you alright?" I whispered, my head carefully against his shoulder.

Dylan coughed a little before wrapping his free arm around me.

"I'll be alright," He spoke. "You?"

I nodded.

I didn't know if we'd ever truly be alright. My head was mush with the overload of emotions that had coursed through me over the last few days. I only prayed that with Dylan by my side, we'd make it out the other end.

He placed a gentle kiss on my forehead before he lay his head against mine.

"That could have gone better," I joked, desperately trying to recover from the tension.

"It could have also been worse," Dylan offered before we both smiled.

As horrid as the turn of events had been there was a slight comfort knowing that everything was now out in the open. Breaking up with our partners was never going to be an easy task. Although I'm sure there were much nicer ways to do it. The pain in Reece's eyes as realisation set in was upsetting to say the very least.

"How long before everyone knows?" I asked Dylan, my fingers stroking circles mindlessly against the taut skin wrapped around his bicep.

"Which part?" He replied and I shuddered.

"Shit, I'm so sorry," I recoiled, "It came out before I even realised what I was saying," I tried to reason.

My mind recalled telling Reece about Dylan's suicide attempt. I shuddered at the memory of finding him and what could have been had I not got here in time. That was only a day ago. So much had changed in such a short space of time.

Dylan placed his index finger against the bow of my upper lip.

"Shh, it's ok. Don't worry about it. People would have probably found out sooner or later," he shrugged seemingly unfazed.

Which struck me as odd because Dylan was a relatively private person and I couldn't imagine him being fine with people knowing one of his darkest and most personal experiences.

"No, it's not OK. I should have known better. Iris can't keep her mouth shut for shit and Reece is so pissed he will probably relay this whole incident to anyone and everyone willing to listen," I could feel myself welling up at the repercussions.

"So let them," Dylan replied coolly.

Both his arms were around me now and he was breathing in my scent. I looked up to meet his eyes completely flummoxed by his nonchalance.

"Look, it's going to be hard having everyone's eyes on us for a while sure, but as long as you're there with me through every step of it I couldn't give a fuck what they think. It's other people's thoughts that had me so worried about shit in the first place and look where that nearly got me," He spoke with a new wisdom and a sincerity in his tone that instantly calmed me.

He was right. As long as we had each other, the opinions of others were of no real interest to me. Not anymore. I was done trying to please the people around me. It was time for us to concentrate on each other.

"So what happens next?" He asked, his hands rubbing up and down my spine.

I leaned back from him and looked him straight in the eyes, a smile playing on my lips.

"Pack your things Dylan," I stated.

His eyebrows knitted.

"You're moving in with me," I smiled.

Dylan's eyebrows furrowed.

Chapter 4

"What?" He asked, mouth still agape.

"Look, let's face it. You hardly spend any time here in your apartment and it's costing you lots of money to keep it going. You haven't fully unpacked any of your belongings and you don't have much furniture. The things you do have are easily transportable to my place. Also, I don't think I will ever be able to shake the bad memories from last night if I come back here. Not to mention thoughts of the time you and Iris have spent here," I shuddered. "So it makes sense for you to come live with me. Don't you think?" I paused.

Dylan just laughed.

"What about the memories I have of Reece in your flat?" He pointed out and I mentally scolded myself.

"You have a point," I sighed.

Shit. I hadn't really thought about that. I was more concerned about the horrid images stuck in my mind of seeing him slumped in the floor. I didn't want my anxiety playing up every time I entered this place and the reminder of not knowing whether or not he had been alive or dead. I couldn't bear the thought of spending much longer in here than necessary and I thought it important to get Dylan out of here too. Maybe we both needed a fresh start. A place of our own to finally call home.

"Well, I mean since you raised some very reasonable points in that speech of yours..." he chuckled.

I blushed.

"Sorry, it's your choice of course. I just, I think it would be good for you. For us," I corrected. "At least temporarily, until you can find somewhere else?" I softened.

He smiled, a warm, heartfelt and genuine gesture.

"I'd love to move in with you," he replied, grabbing my hand and kissing the back of it sweetly.

I beamed.

My stomach was flitting with excitement and nerves. This was really happening. I was going to live with my best friend, not as friends but as boyfriend and girlfriend. Like a real couple with a real future ahead of us. We were going to share our lives together from now on. The thought had me giddy with possibilities.

"What are you thinking about?" Dylan asked, catching me off guard in a little day dream.

"Oh nothing," I grinned.

God I could not keep the smirk from my face.

"Wow, I don't think I've ever seen you smile this much before?" He teased.

My cheeks flushed.

"I can't help it," I chirped, "I'm happy!" I sounded like a little school girl.

Dylan laughed.

"Good! You deserve to be happy," His voice sincere and gravelly, like the tone he always used when he sang.

My body began humming with excitement.

"As do you," I stated coolly.

We both grinned.

Jesus we were like a couple of horny teenagers all over again.

Our hands interlocked and our bodies leaned toward each other. The movement slow and teasing.

"How about we christen this bed one last time before we leave the apartment?" Dylan's offer had my body twisting with impatience.

"I like the sound of that," I breathed, my eyes hazy with lust and longing.

His mouth grazed softly against my lips as his hand tucked my hair behind my ear. This felt like bliss. The kiss deepened and I urged him on, my body craving more of his touch. Dylan kept delaying everything by pulling back teasingly. He broke contact with me three times, torturing me, just as I could feel the heat pulsating between my thighs.

I groaned.

He laughed.

"In fact, I have a proposition," he offered, peppering my cheek and jawline with butterfly kisses.

"Hmm," I responded unable to actually formulate a coherent sentence as his mouth moved further and further until he was kissing me just below my navel.

"Why don't we start looking for a place of our own?" he spoke as he now hurriedly began peeling off my jean shorts and underwear.

My insides were squealing at the sound of him using the term "our" and I could feel my body melting even more beneath the heat of his touch against my skin.

"Deal," I practically yelled, begging for him to continue.

I didn't have to wait long before his tongue was lapping at me down below and I quickly lost track of whatever it was we were even talking about.

I knew right then that Dylan would always get his way with me, but I was more than willing to be compliant.

It only took us three car trips back and forth to completely gut Dylan's flat of his stuff. We left his key in an envelope with the final month's rent payment for the landlord and I waited downstairs while Dylan texted him to confirm that he was moving out. I gave him a moment, knowing he may well have needed it to gather his thoughts.

Sitting there in the car, I ran the last two day's events over in my head. So much drama and pain mixed with so much happiness. It was surreal. My hands were now gripping the steering wheel as I took a deep breath. I hoped that we weren't foolish for rushing in to this. I never really had a doubt in my mind until I contemplated the conversations we still had to have with those around us. I had no idea how my parents would react or Dylan's bandmates. I just knew deep down I couldn't stand the thought of spending another night in that apartment, or Dylan for that matter so him moving in with me seemed perfectly logical. Or so I convinced myself. I caught his frame from the corner of the side mirror and composed myself. There was no turning back now. This was it. The start of it all. A better future for me and him. He crammed himself in to the passenger side, avoiding the mix of black bags and cardboard boxes at his feet.

"You ready?" I asked, turning to face him.

His eyes glistened but he said nothing, simply smiled and nodded.

I started the car and we drove off.

Chapter 5

"And at the end I saw your eyes
As life quietly passed me by
I can't bear to lose you so I'll stay
Live to fight another day
I'll be the one to keep you safe
We'll get the fuck out of this place
We'll make our own escape
Just like we always knew our fate"

It was late Sunday afternoon and the guys had decided to meet up for practice at the pub in town. Dylan had offered me the chance to tag along and since I had the day off work tomorrow, I decided it would be a good way to get to know his band mates a little better. Of course I already knew Trey and Rory over the course of being friends with Dylan the last decade but we had never really hung out just the four of us before and I certainly wasn't close with them by any means. Between work and trying to maintain some resemblance of an adult life I barely had time to attend much social events and as such, often missed out on meeting with the lads.

I listened intently as they jammed acoustically but Dylan's lyrics were almost too painful for me to hear. His voice sounded incredible stripped back but there was no denying the raw emotion in his tone as the words flowed from him.

"Shit Dylan, that works really well," Trey cheered, clearly impressed with their newest songs' developing format.

"You like that huh?" Dylan replied nonchalantly as though he hadn't just poured his very soul in to that last performance.

"For real. People are going to flip for this when we play it live," Trey continued.

Dylan gave him a side smile before looking over at the bar to where I currently sat sipping on my Jack and coke.

"OK, how about we take a break for a while, grab a drink?" Dylan offered to which Rory and Trey agreed.

"Sure thing, I'm just gonna head out for a smoke and I'll meet you at the bar," Rory replied.

"Get me a pint!" He shouted back just before leaving the front door and we all laughed.

Dylan and Trey took a seat at the bar stools either side of me.

"Hey," Dylan whispered as he placed a tender kiss on my cheek.

I still felt like I was floating on air when he kissed me publicly.

"So, what do you think?" Trey interrupted and Dylan elbowed him in the ribs.
"Jesus, sorry!" He rubbed at his side with one hand and called the barmaid over with the other.

"You guys sound great," I replied honestly.

Trey beamed at me before placing his order with the woman at the bar, three pints and another JD for me.

Dylan bopped his head subconsciously along with the music coming from the jukebox behind us. He seemed so relaxed and at ease here. It warmed my heart to see him look close to content. This was the first time I'd ever seen the boys behind the scenes. Their live performances were always intensified by the sound of distorted guitars and heavy vocals. Screaming fans and moshing ultimately distracting my attention from the live show. Granted that was all before Dylan and I had started dating. My job as manager always meant that I had to lock up the restaurant late at night so very rarely I got out in time to actually catch one of their gigs. In fact, I can only recall having seen the boys play live three times, and that was back a few years ago.

Hearing them and seeing them this laid back and in such an informal setting was special for me. I felt like I was privy to some well-guarded secret. It was nice to feel part of something like that. I could see why Dylan spent so much of his free time down here. He seemed to fit in like part of the furniture.

Trey dished out our drinks just as Rory reappeared. He sat next to Dylan, patting him on the shoulder affectionately before sipping on his pint.

"Good job on that last one bro," Rory offered, clinking his glass with Dylan respectively.

"Cheers guys," Dylan held his pint up as we all raised our glasses and took a sip.

"Who was it that came up with the band name?" I asked, curiosity piquing.

"'The Attachment Theory' was all Dylan's contribution," Trey beamed, tilting his glass in appreciation at his bandmate.

"Yep," Dylan smiled, "all me,".

"I never knew that! So what exactly does it mean, in this context," I prompted gesturing my hands toward the three guys.

"It's a well-known psychology term that I learned about years ago in school. It's a theory that makes its basis on the fundamental bonding between a new-born and the relationships they develop with their caregivers. I wanted the name of our band to be routed in connecting us with our fans and the audience on a deeper level. But more like a necessary connection you know like 'The hand that feeds you' sort of thing. Just like a new baby depends on its mother. I wanted people to be able to relate to us and feel like they needed our music. Or at least that's what our main aim was. So yeah, we became The Attachment Theory," he explained.

"Wow," I breathed.

"Yeah," he laughed and his mates did too.

"That's deep," I replied, genuinely surprised by his response. Dylan never ceased to impress.

"That it is," Trey agreed and we all took a moment to let it sink in.

The seriousness quickly waned though as we drank and laughed for a bit, soaking up each other's company. I was happy to hear the stories and jokes between the boys and replied every so often to the odd question thrown my way. The boys were pleasant and hilarious in equal measure and I was thankful that Dylan had them in his life. There was no awkwardness between any of them and I couldn't imagine him managing to find a better suited trio to make music with than these guys. After Dylan confided in the boys a few weeks back about his suicide attempt I knew he feared the possibility of change between them. Sitting here, chatting and listening to them only proved that they were still the same guys, only now they were probably much more attuned to Dylan and that made me relieved. I knew that if there was ever any sign or cause for concern the guys would now be more conscious of it. They had been in a band for over five years now, but I'd never seen them quite as close as they were these days.

"So Lucy, any single friends looking to mingle?" Rory sipped on his third pint now and flexed his eyebrows suggestively to which we all burst out laughing.

Trey nearly spilled half his pint and Dylan threw his hand to his head.

"Here we go," Dylan scoffed as he and Trey exchanged a five pound note between them.

"What the hell? Did you guys bet on me again!" Rory exclaimed.

I looked over to the two boys who were now in hysterics for an explanation.

"Ok guys, let me in on the joke please. Did you bet on Rory asking me that question already?" I queried and both the boys composed themselves enough to respond.

The alcohol was clearly loosening things up.

"Oh we knew he would ask you about your friends," Dylan began, "It was just a matter of when," he explained.

"I bet on three pints, Dylan had five. I won!" Trey cheered raising his glass in the air and downing the lot in one swift gulp.

Rory and Dylan began applauding and so I joined in. Boys were silly sometimes but who was I to upset the novelty between them.

"So..." Rory pressed and laughed this time.

"I'll see what I can do buddy," I clinked his glass and his eyes lit up.

"Get in!" He shouted and we all broke out in fits.

A bit of comic relief to ease the soul. I've had worse Sunday's.

I grinned when Dylan's eyes met mine. He gave me his signature wink, that knowingly devilish charm reminding me of our plans later and I squeezed my knees tighter together in anticipation.

My smile grew wider as he downed his pint and asked the boys if they were ready to head back over to the other side of the bar and continue their rehearsal. They followed his lead, but not before Dylan took a moment to kiss my cheek, his fingertips delicately tracing over my thigh as he whispered in my ear.

My mind went in to overdrive.

He laughed to himself before practically skipping over to the lads and picking up his guitar.

Dylan Wakefield. A gloriously gorgeous human being with one heck of a filthy mouth.

And he was mine.

Chapter 6

DYLAN

We were about two thirds through our set and the atmosphere felt electric. The crowd were really involved and supportive and there was a great buzz around the venue. It felt like we were on the cusp of something big. I paused from the strumming and the singing, turning my back to the crowd momentarily for a sip of my beer. The cool liquid from the bottle eased my throat as it ran down. I looked at Rory, his face half hidden behind his drum kit but I could tell he was bursting with the same excitement as me. I smiled at him knowingly and he clicked his sticks together three times before diving straight in to the beat that would introduce our latest single.

I glanced over at Trey, who was inveigled in an intricate fingerpicking battle with his guitar and watched him nod and wink at the barrage of female fans who had magically appeared before him. I laughed and rolled my eyes before turning back around to face the crowd. My head held high with pride as I stood in front of the mic stand.

I picked up the rhythm riff on my guitar and after a few strums, placed my mouth to the mic and sang.

> *"All you see is love*
> *But all I see is hate*
> *Say you'll meet me halfway*
> *Before it's too late,"*

My eyes cast over the crowd as I punctuated each line with the veracity of a man gone wild. I couldn't keep the shit-eating grin from my face when my eyes pleasantly reflected a sea of people singing each word in sync with me. I felt truly at peace. I had wanted to do this for as long as I could remember and I worked hard to pour every ounce of my being in to every one of my songs. We finally had our target audience and my heart began to swell. We were finally being recognised and taken seriously as a band.

"Got me right where you want me,
With your hands around my throat.
I swear I've had enough of you,
Watch me as I slowly choke."

The voices grew louder and I picked up pace on the strumming. The sweat was almost blinding me but I powered through, adrenaline my saviour.

"Said I wasn't good enough
But what the hell do you know...
I'll make a better life for me
Watch me as I go..."

Trey broke in to his signature glass shattering solo and the crowd flipped. People were moshing and bouncing all over and screaming each word with enough volume to make the amplifiers shake. My heart was pounding in my chest as I ran over to Trey and joined him in his quest to unleash havoc with our instruments.

We hammered the fret boards with our backs pressed against each other, gaining us an unexpected cheer in return. My ego was truly roused and I relished every moment right up until we completed our set.

The crowd were chanting for us long after we had finished playing. Trey, Rory and I hugged each other outside, the smiles from earlier still etched across our faces.

"Fucking hell!" Rory exclaimed as we broke apart.

I couldn't help but laugh.

"I know, right?" I replied, Trey whistling shortly after.

"If only every night was that fucking awesome!" Rory continued.

I loved his enthusiasm. It was moments like these that reminded me of why we set out to do this in the first place. The two guys either side of me had been incredibly supportive during my hardships and they were both super talented. It all seemed worthwhile to feel the high still lingering around us and the expression on their faces. We had accomplished something viable and concrete tonight. I would never forget this moment.

We were almost done loading the van with our gear when a whistle from behind caught our attention. A small group of about four girls were waving and beckoning us over. Rory clapped his hands together with delight and Trey politely waved back.

"Come on then lads," Rory began, "Let's reap our rewards shall we?" He began marching toward the girls who were soon throwing their arms around him and kissing him on the cheek.

I smiled to myself and told Trey to join him and that I would catch up with them in a minute. He patted me respectively on the shoulder telling me to meet him inside when I was done. I gave him the thumbs up before slamming the side door of the van shut and jumping in to the passenger seat.

Reaching in to the side pocket of my jeans, I grabbed my mobile. Scanning the screen, I saw a text from Lucy;

"Hey dude! Running late (as usual) but will catch up with you at the bar around 11pm. Hope the gig went well, can't wait to see you xxx"

Checking the time which read 10.17pm, I quickly responded;

"The gig was incredible, Best one yet. Wish you had been here. No problem babe, see you soon xxx"

I frowned, feeling a little saddened that I couldn't share my current euphoria with Lucy in greater detail. I knew that she was a hard worker but I often wished she had the chance to actually catch one of our live sets instead of hearing me speak about it afterwards. There were some moments you just could not relay in words.

Shoving my momentary downer to the back of my mind, I vacated the van and headed back to the club's entrance. Rory was still surrounded by seemingly appreciative new female fans. I high-fived him as I approached and then went in search of Trey inside. I had barely made it past the cloakroom doorway when a tap on the shoulder made me spin around.

A short, dark haired girl...who looked around sixteen was nervously gazing up at me. I furrowed my brow in such a manner, trying to place as to whether or not I recognised her.

"Hi, umm, sorry to bother you and all but I wondered if I could possibly use some pictures I took of you guys tonight for my college project?" The girl spoke fast and her words ran together in one elongated sentence.

My eyes raked over the strap around her neck and the huge DLR camera hanging from it. She had a piece of paper in one hand and a pen in the other but she could barely maintain eye contact with me. I suddenly felt an urge to protect her, as if she were some fragile little thing.

"Sure!" I replied as enthusiastically as I could, "Need me to sign something?" I suggested, pointing to the waiver I could just make out from beneath her fingertip.

"Please," She beamed, clearly relieved at my response as she passed me the pen and paper eagerly.

I leaned against the cloakroom door and scribbled my initials on the dotted line. Handing the items back to the girl I studied her for a moment. She had dark framed glasses that perched perfectly on the bridge of her nose and matched the colour of her hair. Her eyes were deep brown and her skin alabaster pale. She wore a dark grey hoodie and ripped jeans. She was cute but in a geeky sort of way. We exchanged smiles before she began heading back towards the exit.

"Wait up!" I cried and she spun around surprised.

"What's your name?" I asked suddenly out of impulse.

She sheepishly hugged her camera before responding.

"Iris," She stated shyly, tucking a hair behind her ear and scooting her glasses up a notch.

"Nice to meet you Iris. Good luck with the college project," I smiled again, hoping that I didn't come across as some total creep.

"Thanks. Good luck with the album," She beamed and then headed off again.

I grinned in appreciation. It felt good to have fans. I playfully slapped the door three times before practically skipping to the bar. It was time to celebrate with my fellow bandmates.

Chapter 7

August 2000

Me and the boys had been backstage for around an hour in preparation for tonight's headline slot. The support acts had been generous enough to provide us with a couple of cases of beer so we had no need to go back and forth to the bar all night. It felt odd spending the evening hidden away from the crowd but there was a comfort in knowing that it meant bigger things were coming our way. We were due to arrive on stage in the next fifteen minutes so I decided to nip outside for a quick smoke. As I exited the back of the venue and headed towards the door my eyes caught sight of Iris, casually leaned against a support pillar, studying her camera. I smiled to myself, grateful that she was here. It was always a pleasant feeling having someone familiar in times like these.

As though she sensed my presence, her eyes flicked up toward me, her eyes alight as if she too was pleased to see me. I smiled, giving her a polite nod before heading for the door. There was little time to spare before our set.

The next hour and forty- five minutes went by in a flash. We played our debut EP in full and a few covers to warm up the crowd. We strummed and sang until our fingers hurt and our voices grew hoarse. It was the first time we'd played so hard and so energetically for a long time. The crowd lapped up every morsel, cheering and screaming in sync with each track. The surreal, shuddering sound of stamping feet tore through the paper thin walls and enforced us to come back for an encore. Having run out of tracks to play, we settled for a repeat of our hit single and a cover of 'Ballroom Blitz'. The crowd went ape-shit, as did we. I felt liberated in a way I had never felt before. Exhausted and out of songs, Trey, Rory and I thanked the crowd before retreating once more back stage.

The back stage area consisted of a table laden with beer and a couple of comfortable couches. The guys from the two support bands were waiting when we arrived with drinks in hand, sloshing beer from their half drunken bottles and cheering enthusiastically.

"Fuckin' hell lads you smashed it!" Seth, the bassist cried hugging Trey, seemingly dumbstruck with awe.

"Incredible performance mate, the crowd really went nuts for that last cover!" Mike slurred a little, clearly having had a good few beverages.

"Cheers guys!" Rory thanked the boys, clinking beer bottles with a few of us.

The three of us grabbed some more beers and settled on a couch in the back. The sweat was dripping from my forehead by this point, only made worse with the thick summer heat. The three bands crammed up in here only made the stifling warmth much worse. I never did handle confined spaces very well and felt a sudden urge to seek some reprieve.

"I'm going to head out for a smoke guys, be back in a minute," I shook Trey's hand and gave Seth and Mike a polite nod as I passed.

The minute I stepped outside the room I instantly felt better and gulped in a huge breath of fresher air.

"Are you alright?" A small voice beckoned.

Iris came in to my line of vision then, camera still in hand and those dark framed glasses perfectly hitched up the bridge of her nose. Her hair was tied back loosely, leaving one or two tendrils beside both ears. Her pale complexion was a stark contrast to the darkness of her eyes. There was no denying that she was gorgeous though.

My lips parted and I breathed out once more.

"Yeah, of course! It's just fucking sweltering in there so I'm headed out for some fresh air. Care to join?" I offered, gesturing my hand toward a little side entrance that was predominantly used as a fire exit.

"Okay," She smiled.

She brushed past me ever so slightly and hit the bar to release the door, a cool wisp of the freshest air blowing in from outside. I followed her lead and let the breeze whip around my face and hair. The door closed behind us.

"Fuck that feels good," I stretched out my arms and let the cool air continue its onslaught across my chest and armpits.

My t-shirt was drenched from my sweat and I was in desperate need of a shower. I raked my hand over my forehead in a meek attempt to dry it a little, suddenly conscious of the mess I was in. I reached in to my jean pocket and pulled out my pack of cigarettes. I offered the pack to Iris but she politely shook her head in a decline. I sparked one up for myself, sheltering the flame from the passing wind.

Smoking was one of the bad habits I had inherited since being around the guys more often. I used to hate it when I was younger but now, it gave me the best excuse to escape.

Iris was leaned against the wall, her eyes looking to me somewhat in request of conversation and a small smile playing across her lips.

"What?" I asked, taking a long drag and letting the smoke fill my lungs.

"Nothing," She grinned harder this time.

"Say what's on your mind," I urged, smiling curiously.

"It's just you said you wanted some fresh air, yet you're stood there smoking," She giggled and I swear it was the cutest fucking sound I'd heard all night.

"Haha, yeah, I didn't really think that one through," I rolled my eyes and laughed at my contradicting nature.

Iris had the heel of one converse shoe pressed against the brick wall and her hands nestled inside her hoodie pockets. Her camera slung haphazardly around her neck as she leaned her head back against the wall, her eyes gazing across the sky at the setting sun.

"What did you think of tonight then?" I asked, taking another draw and pressing myself against the wall to her left.

The view was always great at this time of night. The little side entrance here had been an old favourite of mine. The bar's owner had been the one who had shown it to me a couple of years back. I had promised to keep its use to a minimum to avoid breaking any laws but tonight it was one of the furthest things in my mind. I was grateful for the little sanctuary and for my unexpected company. I'd never even shown this to Lucy and I considered her my best friend.

"You guys were on fire, like literally. Everyone was hooked and I don't think I've ever seen you guys play so hard before," her voice was full of genuine admiration and at the same time she sounded much quieter now, as if the close proximity had her shying away.

"Hence the sweaty mess I'm in," I joked and she smiled.

That smile was too cute for words. She had the sweetest little crook in her cheek each time she did but she barely held my eyes for longer than a second each time she spoke. I'd never conversed with a girl who suffered from such coyness before. It was intriguing and alluring all the same. I wanted to unravel her a little and possibly find out a bit more about her. She wasn't intentionally mysterious but much more reserved than most other girls we'd meet. Our band had developed a few over eager followers in more recent years. Not that Trey and Rory seemed to mind. They always did have a much easier time with the ladies than I did.

"Did you get some good shots then?" I pointed at the large black device she carried with her, her hands quickly clasping over the object like it was the most precious thing she had ever held.

"Sure, I got some good pictures yeah," She blushed then and I felt a twitch in my groin.

Fuck this girl was adorable.

"Can I see?" I dropped my cigarette to the ground and pressed on it with my battered DC's.

The red in her cheeks only intensified as she nodded and I leaned closer to her, trying to get a look on the viewfinder screen. Her hands deftly flicked a switch at the right of the camera so that the last few images appeared on the LCD display screen. She scrolled past them, silent as she showcased her work. A close up image of me, veins protruding from my arms and neck as I screamed in to the microphone and hammered on the guitar strings. She had somehow managed to encapsulate me completely lost in the moment, capturing the intensity beautifully.

"Fucking hell Iris, these are incredible!" I couldn't disguise how utterly impressed I was with her photography skills.

She shrugged and then clicked the side of the camera again, the still image disappearing and leaving a blank screen in its place. Her cheeks were still glowing from her obvious discomfort at having her work scrutinised.

"Seriously, you should get them published or something," I offered, stepping back from her while trying to gauge her face. She placed her feet back on the solid ground and shoved her hands back in her pockets nervously, her eyes casting downward.

"It's no big deal, just going to use them for some college work that's all," She mumbled, clearly unaware of the raw talent she held.

"What's it like, taking pictures?" I asked, desperate to unveil some more thoughts that were clearly running through her mind.

Her head raised, her eyes boring in to mine, comforted I guessed that I was still showing an interest in her work. Photography was clearly a passion of hers and her talent was undeniable. I genuinely wanted to hear more about it.

"How does it feel, you mean?" She goaded, squinting her eyes a little as she spoke.

"Yeah, what does it feel like when you're taking those," I pointed to her camera.

She grabbed the device again with both hands, let out a deep sigh and smiled. Her actions told me that she clearly found the entire process of utmost importance. I crossed my arms over my chest and gave her the time she needed to put it in to words. My chest was suddenly expanding with sheer curiosity and a spreading warmth that I could not pin down. Maybe it was the beer or the setting sun.

"It's hard to explain," She began, her cheeks tinged pink again with my bestowed focus on her answer.

"When I look at things through my lens, I feel a sense of superiority. Like, I'm in charge of how things will go with my next shot. Everything and everyone has two sides. A good side and a bad side. It's up to me to decide which side I want to focus on, which side I want to showcase".

Her eyes were alive now as she spoke each word, her focus on me as if she were trying to decide internally whether or not I would understand her depiction, or perhaps decipher whether I was good or bad. The truth is, her words resonated with me in a much deeper and moral way. She basically described life in a few short sentences. I smiled. I knew there was a reason I liked this girl. She had real depth and not just the kind you see through a lens.

"Anyways," She shied away, her coy demeanour quickly returning, "I guess I just like the feeling of being in control every once in a while," she sighed.

My head quickly drifted to a dirty thought of her being dominant in the bedroom but I stifled it away.

"I get that," I nodded, trying to compose myself.

What was with this girl and her effect on me? Just then, the side entrance door flew open and Rory came spilling out with two blonde girls either side. I erupted with laughter straight away knowing that this was my drummer's idea of heaven and I was never going to hear the end of this.

"Party's back inside lads, what the fuck are you doing out here?" He slurred, looking from me to Iris while both girls either side began giggling and toying with his checked shirt.

"I'll just be a minute," I teased, escorting the three buds back towards the door.

Rory winked at Iris muttering "Oi, oi!" as he and his two lady friends retreated back inside.

"Lucy and Reece will be here soon," Rory spoke and I nodded.

"Yeah she texted me buddy, will be in soon I promise," I pleaded.

I glanced at Iris, shaking my head apologetically. She gave me that killer smile again and tucked her hair behind her ear.

"I guess you better go back to your friends," She spoke, her voice tinged with a sort of sadness which tugged at me in ways I can't explain.

"Why don't you come join us?" I offered, one hand holding the door open.

I wasn't ready for my time with her to be over just yet.

"I'm sorry, I can't," She sheepishly replied, but she never proceeded to give me an explanation as to why not and I never pressed her on it.

"I can always stay out here with you if you prefer?" I knew deep down that ditching my band mates and my best friend on a night where we'd just performed a killer show was a complete dick move but I wanted to prove to Iris that there was more to me than what she probably perceived.

"Don't be daft, go inside and have fun. I have to go home and edit these pictures for class anyways," she tried her best shot at a genuine smile but I could sense she hadn't wanted our encounter to end either.

"I'll see you around though, yeah?" I tried to sound casual about it but I was determined to get to know more about her.

"Sure, I'd like that," and just like that the spark in her eyes grew wild with sincerity and my stomach felt knotted.

"Take care of yourself," my voice sounded much deeper and way more authoritative than I had intended.

"You too, *Dad,*" she chimed sarcastically before disappearing toward the gate at the end of the car park.

The girl had spunk, I just needed to coax it from her. Staring at her figure from behind, I watched her until she faded in to the darkness before turning back inside and reuniting myself with my fellow bandmates.

Chapter 8

Nine months later, our band finally had more airplay and became a regular feature on the radio. The remaining tour dates had all sold out and the gigs were some of the best nights I'd ever spent in my entire life. The first album was completed and ready for release any day now. Juggling a full time job in a call centre and a part time job as a rock-star had taken its toll though. I had used a two-week holiday from work to travel with the boys to a few different cities and towns across country and left no time to recuperate on our return before slogging it back in the office. My mind was reeling with the mundane task of answering call after call having just spent some real time doing the one thing I loved the most. This job merely gave me enough cash to pay my own household bills and I used whatever I could spare to pay for recording time and buying new equipment. Sharing my internal heartache with other citizens of the world who were willing to pay money to come to our shows and actually having a good fucking time was my main objective. Some days this world felt bleak, but sharing those thoughts with others through my music had helped counteract a balance. I actually got a buzz from the entire thing. I didn't want to do anything else. Live performances like the ones we'd just done would always be my first love.

Speaking of love, my mind began filtering through the memory of seeing Iris at one of our hometown shows. I hadn't seen her since then and that fact irked me something vicious. It was as if she had disappeared from the face of the Earth. Granted we hadn't played here in a while but I spent most of my weekends hanging out with the lads and still never caught a glimpse of her. Although she didn't strike me as the partying type. Not that there was anything wrong with that of course, I just sensed it by her reaction toward the girls she'd seen Rory with that night she showed me some of her pictures. Her mood had changed the second they'd come through the door.

As my mind wandered back to that night, I started trying to come up with a way to find her. I didn't dare text Lucy for fear of being ribbed as some kind of creep. I'm pretty sure she had social media, I mean who the hell doesn't these days but I didn't want to come across as a total stalker. I also always found the whole sharing of everything in such a public manner completely horrid. Yes, I know, Ironic coming from someone who openly spills their guts on stage for a living, but my platform had always felt more real than a few lines written across a screen. Social media was the death of real social interaction. People no longer had to stray from their homes to feel close to their favourite stars or relay a memory with a friend. A quick check on Twitter or a photo shared on Facebook took care of everything. I missed having friends call around to your door and actually conversing in person. God, I made myself sound like such an old man sometimes. That reminds me. I'm twenty-one next month.

I sighed, breathing so heavily in to the headset I caused a little feedback to vibrate against my ears. I stared up from the screen to watch the second hand of the clock on the wall in front tick by. It was only two forty pm but I had already had enough for the day. Closing my eyes and placing my head in my hands, I breathed out once more. Surely there was more to life than sitting in this shitty ass office all day?

Frustrated with knowing I still had a good three hours to work before I could get home, I began searching for the local college's website. There was only one college situated in our town and I hoped that there may be some way for me to track down more information on Iris. Yes, I am aware that seems a little extreme considering the fact I don't even know the girls last name, but I could not get her out of my head. I had no last name and didn't know her age for sure. I pondered that for a while. The webpage was bog standard and droned on about some upcoming fundraising event that was being held this weekend. I quickly scrolled through the home page in search of more information when the sight of her grabbed my attention. There, on the screen in front was Iris. Her hair was tousled over her shoulders, her signature glasses shielding her eyes as she was snapped shaking the hand of an elderly gentleman dressed in a grey suit.

I squinted at the screen again, to be sure but there was no mistaking it. It was her. I read the caption beneath the image that was featured in the article.

"Local girl Iris wins prestigious award for her photography submission in community college project,".

I beamed with pride, smiling to myself. I knew the girl had talent and I was so glad someone was paying tribute to that. My fingers quickly scrolled further, eager to see what else had been written.

"Iris Steadman, 17, has been awarded for her effort during a photography project that asked students to capture a variety of emotions. Iris provided the community college with a series of seven images entitled "Cardinal Vices", a conceptual piece which featured pictures of people depicting acts associated with each of the seven deadly sins; Pride, Greed, Lust, Envy, Gluttony, Wrath and Sloth. Her teacher, Boris Caldwell recommended Iris's work after her submission to his project left him "dumfounded and awed" at her individual take on the task.

Here you can see some examples of her work;"

My fingers scrolled to an image of an obese woman sitting on a park bench her mouth wrapped around a baguette that had sandwich filling dripping over her fingertips. The still captured the moment precisely with its intent; a depiction of gluttony as was captioned underneath the article image.

My fingers continued to scroll a little further until the next image stopped me dead in my tracks. I gasped, my heart pulsating when I realised the person I was looking at was me. It was a shot from the gig we'd first played here, the one where we'd spoken briefly for the very first time and she'd nervously asked me to sign a waiver for use of her pictures. She'd never actually shown me the images she'd taken from that night and my dumbass had been too slow to ask. I stared at the image. My eyes were focused on the crowd, my smile stretched to the farthest corners of my face and my hands splayed outwards in an almost Jesus Christ-esque pose. The image had been altered to a black and white filter and everything besides me in the shot had been blurred. The caption underneath read 'Pride'.

I paused for a moment, feeling a mixture of complete flattery, yet a little prejudice. Is that what she thought of me? Her attention to detail was remarkable though and the image itself made for a powerful message. I leaned back in my chair, incredulously taken aback by my discovery.

"Fuck me," I muttered, shaking my head in disbelief.

One of my co-workers looked over in disgust, obviously offended at my vulgar language.

"Sorry," I smiled but she rolled her eyes and looked away.

I raised my middle finger in frustration and aimed it at her back. Childish I know, but it made me feel better about myself for a second. Slouching back in my chair and sighing again for the umpteenth time, I decided it was best to get back to work. The mystery of Iris Steadman and my hunt for her whereabouts would just have to wait a little longer. Well, at least until I'd finished my shift.

Chapter 9

June 2001

On the way home from work, I stopped in by the local corner store to grab some pasta and a jar of Bolognese for supper. Living alone had its perks, I guess. I could always be last minute with my decisions and it was relatively cheap to live off ready-made or quick foods. Not so sure my health would agree with my current eating lifestyle but I would face that battle another day. If I lived that long of course. I was just about to pay for my goods when the little bell above the door rang, signalling a new customer. I instinctively looked across the dried pasta shelves and in the direction of the doorway. Holy fuck. It was her. Iris. Iris Steadman. The phantom photographer. Iris came in, wireless headphones engulfing her ears, signature spectacles perched just right and her dark hair flowing over her shoulders. She had a rucksack on her back and was headed for the fridge aisle. My heart jittered with a new buzz at seeing her here, in such an ordinary environment and outside of a dimly lit venue. This was it. This was my chance.

Placing my items hurriedly down on the shelf in front of me, I dashed for the freezers in a bid to catch her attention. She seemed caught up in her own little word as she bopped her head carefree, clearly enjoying whatever she was listening to. I leaned against the furthest away fridge and smiled, crossing my arms over my chest and just enjoyed watching her. She was currently scanning the well-stocked variety of energy juice's. Seemingly settled on a giant tin of Red Bull, she slammed the door behind her and made toward where I stood. Her eyes raised and when she saw me there she froze. I winked at her as she pulled hear headphones down so they now slung around her neck.

"Dylan!" She almost yelled, clearly surprised.

"Hey stranger, " I teased before straightening myself up.

Her cheeks quickly flushed pink again and I grinned. She was the cutest, truly.

"What you up to?" I offered seeing as she was struggling to come up with anything.

"I uhh, I was just about to edit some shots for class," She bashfully replied, twisting the can of fizzy energy nervously.

"Cool, how's that going by the way?" I played dumb, knowing fine well she'd been receiving some great recognition for her work lately.

"Good, yeah," She smiled, "Really well actually. People seem to like what I do," She beamed.

"That's great!" I replied enthusiastically, "And why shouldn't they. You clearly have the knack for it," I stated. It was true.

She shrugged sheepishly, her gaze lowered and fixated on her black and white converse.

I felt compelled to break down her walls brick by brick. The girl was clearly affected by me and I hoped that was a good sign. I certainly hadn't managed to get her from my mind since we'd last spoken. I was itching to find out more about her. Knowing it was a little forward but feeling brave nonetheless, I spoke again.

"Listen, if you don't have any dinner plans, fancy coming over to mine so we can order pizza or Chinese food and hang out for a bit?" There, I'd said it. There was no going back now.

She stared up at me, her mouth physically agape.

"You, you want me to come over? To your place?" Her voice was a miniscule moment away from trembling.

"Sure, why not? You can tell me about college and photography and I can bore you with the details of our last few shows. Besides, it's Friday night, do you really want to spend it glued to a computer screen all night?" I may have been trying too hard to sound compelling but it felt important for me to get to know this girl.

Besides, I hated being alone in my apartment and Trey and Rory were off visiting some friends and family in Scotland this weekend.

She studied me once more, as if to check that I was being sincere and not playing a prank on her before responding.

"Ok, but you're buying, I'm a poor student after all," She grinned and it was my turn for my mouth to fall open, struck dumb by the zest of cheekiness she managed to conjure up as she went to pay for her Red Bull.

This girl was going to be the death of me.

Chapter 10

The walk to my apartment only took around five minutes so the conversation had been kept to a minimum. I keyed in the code to unlock the flat door and held it open before ushering Iris inside. We took two flights of stairs until we reached my apartment door and I unlocked it with haste.

"Cool place," Iris offered as she surveyed the room.

I knew she was just trying to be polite because truthfully it was nothing to look at. I'd spent a little over a year living in here and had yet to fully unpack the dust covered boxes which held most of my prised belongings. The walls were bare except for a vinyl record clock I had hung up in the kitchen area, a housewarming gift from Lucy and I had almost nothing in the way of furniture.

"Thanks," I muttered nonchalantly, "But you don't have to lie to me," I teased.

She blushed, knowing she'd been caught out and somehow it made me giddy again to see her reaction.

"Did you just move in?" She pondered, her finger deftly tracing over some of the boxes.

"About a year ago," I laughed.

She giggled too and my smile grew wide.

"Grab a seat by the window," I gestured to the tiny, grey couch.

She sat softly, folding her legs underneath her as she did so. Her backpack was placed on the floor beside her and she cracked open her tin of Red Bull before taking a long sip.

I grabbed the bean bag from the corner of the room and placed it a little away from her. I slouched down taking a seat on the bean filled cushion so that I was facing her.

"What are you in the mood for?" I asked, removing my mobile from my pocket so that I could order takeaway.

"Chinese sounds good," She spoke, her eyes on me.

I nodded before hurriedly typing some keys in to my device.

"Awesome, any preferences?"

"Surprise me," She beamed.

I tilted my head to look at her and raised my eyebrows in a suggestive manner.

She blushed.

"You got it," I nodded, the biggest smile on my face.

I couldn't resist teasing this girl. She was so easy to wind up.

I tapped at the keys a bit more furiously this time, eagerly completing the online food order so that I could get back to what was more important.

"There. It says it should be about twenty minutes for delivery," I clicked my phone screen off and shoved the device back in to my jean pocket.

"Cool, how much do I owe you?" She began filtering through her backpack in search of her purse.

"My treat remember?" I insisted.

"I don't mind, I was only kidding around before," She continued rummaging when some pictures fell from the pack and scattered across the floor.

I automatically leapt forward to aid her in picking up the spilled contents. Tonnes of prints and still images caught my attention and I couldn't help but study them a little closer. The particular one in my hand was a snap of two girls, they looked around Iris's age. Only these girls were full on

French-kissing and had their legs overlapping each other while they both sat under a silver monument.

 "Wow," I breathed, caught off guard.

"Sorry, it's not what you think. It's for a project I'm working on," She quickly snatched the pictures from my hand and stuffed them back in her backpack, her unease evident as her cheeks burned.

"Iris, it's cool, you don't have to worry about that sort of thing with me. I'm no prude. Besides, it's a great picture. Did you take that shot," I was on my knees now, beside her as she tucked some hair behind her ears and zipped up the backpack.

"Yeah," She spoke timidly, her nervous hands rubbing against her thighs in an attempt to smooth out her black fitted jeans.

"What kind of project you working on?" I prompted, knowing she felt uncomfortable but making it my duty to allow her to be herself around me.

"It's silly," She began but I placed my hand on her shoulder reassuringly.

"It's not silly, please," I gave her a little squeeze and she took in a sharp breath.

Her eyes found mine again and she breathed out. I removed my hand from her shoulder, sat down on the couch she had been on earlier and patted the space next to me.

"Please," I repeated. "I don't bite, well, unless you're in to that sort of thing," I joked and the tension immediately dispersed.

Iris picked herself up from the floor, and casually plunked herself down next to me on the couch. She took another sip of from her can, offering it to me but I politely shook my head. Energy juice would have only made me more jittery and I was already a little on edge. She began;

"It's just a project at school. There's a theme, 'emotions'. We have to capture images that convey various emotions. The one you saw, the two girls? I called that one 'Lust," She finished, her eyes darting around the room.

"Incredible," I breathed, knowing all along about her so called 'project' after my slightly invasive yet extensive search for her on the college web page earlier.

"Are they friends of yours?" I asked suddenly and she shook her head swiftly.

"What? No, no they are two complete random people I happened to see one day on my way home from one of your gigs actually," She continued. "I asked them to sign a waiver too though, like you did, so I'm not doing anything without the correct permission," she stated proud of herself.

I smiled, nodding in understanding.

"You in to that sort of thing?" I asked bluntly.

It was out before I'd even realised how ridiculous I sounded.

"What, kissing girls?" She asked coolly.

She had better nerve than I gave her credit for.

"Yeah," I straightened up a little.

"Not really, at least I don't think so," She blushed and I pondered her statement for a while.

"Surely you'd know by now if you were though right? I mean you're what, seventeen, eighteen?" I asked, clearly giving no regard to boundaries considering we hardly knew each other.

Her cheeks burned again and she physically squirmed in her seat.

"Umm, I guess yeah," She sipped the cool drink again, her eyes on the sitting room door.

"Sorry Iris, I didn't mean to make you uncomfortable, I'm just trying to get to know you better," I offered.

The last thing I wanted to do was scare her off. Maybe I was being too forward with the girl. There was just something about her I couldn't get enough of.

"It's cool, I'm sorry if I seem weird I'm just a little embarrassed that's all," She smiled this time and looked me dead in the eye as she spoke.

I was torn between thinking this girl was devastatingly shy one minute and then dangerously curious and courageous the next.

"What the hell do you have to be embarrassed about? I'd never judge you for your sexuality, I hoped you'd think better of me than that," I feigned, feeling a little hurt that she would think so little of me.

"No, no it's not that," She stuttered. "I mean, I don't think I'm gay but I wouldn't actually know because I've never actually been...," she paused.

"With a girl?" I added.

"With anyone," she corrected.

Her eyes flicked up to me once more looking for my reaction.

I frowned a little, trying to process this information. A Virgin? I raised my eyebrows in surprise.

"What?" She laughed.

"Nothing, wow. I mean, that's just, wow." I laughed.

"See, it IS embarrassing!" She slammed her palms against her face and audibly groaned.

"No, it's not! It's something you should be proud of! I'm just super surprised that's all. But in a good way," I reassured her by placing my hand on her knee.

"Why because you thought I was a slut?!" She tensed and it was my turn to groan.

"No! I know you're not like other girls. You're just the opposite in fact," I tried to reason, my hand still touching her.

She peeked from between her fingertips that were currently shielding her eyes at my hand placed on her knee.

I breathed out and then removed my hand, slowly. She removed her hands from her face and met my eyes, clearly trying to process a thought.

I looked back at her and offered a smile, a genuine one that was truly heartfelt. I may not have been as innocent as Iris but I was far from a man whore and I had respect for women who had respect in themselves. Being in the music industry had taught me a few life lessons about the kinds of girls this world had created and girls like Iris were few and far between. I was just about to open my mouth when the buzzer went.

"That will be the food," I grinned and Iris smiled.

I think we both welcomed the break in the tension between us with utter relief. I was also grateful for a distraction from our earlier conversation. I certainly hadn't intended for our words to veer off in the direction they did. However, it felt good to have Iris confide in me with a personal fact about her. It made me feel a little closer to the girl and that was my honest intention for tonight. That and not wanting to spend the night alone. I really did hate being in my apartment by myself.

We plated up the delicious warm food and scoffed two thirds of the generous portion sizes while talking. We mostly talked about interests and hobbies, music, art and our favourite films. We both loved the horror genre and spent a great deal of our youth being teased for looking like goths. Iris still got teased about it at her college to this day. I hadn't been subjected to that kind of teasing for a few years now since I was a little older. Well at least not from other kids. My mother's boyfriend on the other hand, well that was a different story. We touched on our family, Iris stating she had two younger sisters and lived with her mother and father at home and I told her that I was an only child and had left my mother's house last year when I turned twenty. It was easier that way. The less she knew about my family the better. It was far too sensitive a topic for a first introduction. My family had brought me nothing but grief since my sister passed away years ago.

All in all, the night had been a success and Iris seemed much more open and relaxed around me now that we had taken the time to get to know one another a little better and the conversation had been much more chilled. And just like that, the chatter diverted back on to more personal topics.

"So, you don't have a girlfriend?" Iris asked, twisting a vegetable spring roll between her thumb and forefinger.

"Nah," I replied nonchalantly while sipping on my bottle of beer.

"How come," She pressed, those dark, innocent eyes boring in to me.

I shrugged. How could I even begin to explain my reasoning? I always kept things casual because I couldn't deal with the pressure that came with having a girlfriend. There were always too many questions and expectations and I knew deep down I would fail them miserably because of my troubled past. A past that was destined to come back and bite me in the ass every so often. It's not that I didn't love the idea of having someone by my side, I just couldn't bear the idea of hurting someone I loved unintentionally. Love brought pain. I never knew any better. Besides I wasn't sure what love was. I'd only ever found solace in the sack. Sex and split. That was how I usually rolled.

She bit down on the spring roll delicately. If I hadn't known any better, I'd have thought she was trying to tease me intentionally.

I cleared my throat. Now it was my turn to feel a little uneasy. Deciding it was time to throw the ball back in to the court I decided to do some questioning of my own.

"How come you never had a boyfriend before?" I pressed, swallowing again from the bottle and grinning like mad.

Iris laughed.

"Or girlfriend?" She teased.

"Exactly!" I cheered, clinking my bottle with her glass as she sipped on some Pepsi.

She took two large gulps before setting her glass down. She scooted back on the couch and sighed.

"It's not like I planned to remain a virgin at this age," She began. "It's just there really hasn't ever been an opportunity that presented itself," She sighed again but smiled this time.

I stared at her incredulously.

"You're lying," I spoke, shifting my weight so that my entire body was poised to look at her now from the couch.

"I'm not! No one has ever seemed that interested in me. Ever. All through school I was teased for being a goth or having glasses. By the time I hit puberty everyone was already hooking up with someone else and I just buried myself in photography. It was my little sanctuary to escape the hardships of mean girls and guys who used to take the piss out of me for being different. I learned to block out the insults and one day they eventually stopped. The sad thing was it was like everyone just forgot about me or grew bored of it all. I very much became a loner after that and so no one ever really approached me," she explained.

My heart felt pained at the discomfort she had endured. I too knew loneliness. It was fucking awful.

"Fuck," I breathed out.

"Yeah," she mumbled.

"No one ever came close enough, or even put in the effort to get to know me. Except for you, of course," She smiled at me then, her gorgeous dark eyes rimmed with a sheen of clear liquid that took my breath away.

How was it possible that no one had seen the utter beauty blossoming in this girl before me?

"How could I not want to get to know you," I began. "You're incredibly talented and smart and undeniably beautiful. The world is riddled with fools if they dare consider to think otherwise," I stated.

Her mouth fell open slightly at my words.

"What?" I prompted.

She blushed.

"You called me beautiful,"

"That's because you are".

"No one's ever said that to me before," her cheeks were almost scarlet now.

"That's because people are dicks," I confirmed and she laughed.

She tucked another strand of hair behind her ear and brought her finger up to her lower lip, caressing it slowly. I was already struggling to compose myself in such close proximity when she spoke suddenly.

"Can I confess something to you," it was almost a whisper.

"Anything".

"I really want to kiss you right now".

My heart started pounding.

"Then do it," I offered.

Her eyes grew wide in obvious surprise with my response. I wanted it badly too but I knew this all had to be on her terms. She was young, a virgin and I didn't want her to feel pressured in any way. Like I said, I was no saint by any means but I had values and a moral code that I rarely fought against.

She shifted a little closer, clearly trying to pluck up the courage to follow through. I kept my hands pinned to my thighs so that she had full control.

"But I'm nervous," She whispered, her breath inches from my face.

"Don't be," I replied huskily.

She closed her eyes then and drifted forward, slowly, her lips lining up to meet my own.

She placed a soft, gentle kiss at first, her hand pressed against my chest to prevent her from falling forward too much. Her knees were pushed against mine on the couch as she leaned over, eyes still prised shut as she let the kiss linger for a moment. I held perfectly still.

After another brief moment had passed, she opened her eyes and stared directly at me. Her cheeks flared and she leaned back.

"I...I don't really know what I'm doing," she blushed, nervously playing with the rim of her black t-shirt.

Her innocence and complete lack of knowledge in this department had me absolutely astounded. I was a gentleman deep down though and wanted to make sure she felt no shame in her actions and she had every right to feel empowered. She was beautiful and I knew there was confidence hiding in there somewhere.

"You're doing fine," I grinned, placing my hand on the side of her cheek in a bid to comfort her.

"Do you mind if I give you some pointers though?" I offered gently as not to hurt her feelings.

She nodded enthusiastically and I felt a twitch in my groin. Shoving that thought to the farthest part of my mind I composed myself. I was not going to rush in to this. I would make sure Iris could trust me and had a little more experience in the field before it ever came to the main event, if it ever came down to that. A little voice in my head goaded me that it would, in time.

"Okay," I breathed. "First, you want to be as close as possible, and comfy. So, why don't you sit on my lap?" I asked and her eyes grew wide.

"Don't panic, we aren't rushing in to anything that you don't want. It's just for kissing, I promise," I reassured her and patted my thighs respectively.

Iris carefully slung her legs over mine and positioned herself above me. I lowered my hands on to her hips to steady her in place and breathed out before I spoke.

"Put your hands around my neck," and she did so without question.

"Now, this time when you kiss me, keep your lips parted slightly as you do and hold it in place a little longer. Kiss me as many times as you feel comfortable and each time you do, my lips will follow suit to yours, so don't freak out ok?" she nodded in understanding.

I breathed once more, feeling her breath against me as she closed her eyes and neared me.

Her lips found mine and this time, came with a little more force. I kissed her back this time too, my mouth meeting each of her little kisses in succession and moving together almost in sync. The string of individual kisses eventually grew into longer, continuous kissing until our lips almost felt as if they were one and the same.

I pulled back momentarily to gain my composure again, feeling my hard on pushing against the material of my jeans.

"Right, good," I praised, my smile stretching wider and my eyes burning with desire.

"Was that okay?" Iris asked, her lips looking fuller and her eyes peering at me over her glasses with eager anticipation.

"You're doing incredible," and she grinned, exposing that cute little crinkle set deep in her cheek.

"If you want, I can teach you one more thing tonight," I offered and she hesitated, her arms still wrapped around my neck and mines still holding tightly to her hips.

"Don't worry, we're still in the kissing faze," I teased and she eased down on me with a giggle.

"I promised I wouldn't push you," I stated and she nodded.

"Okay, I want you to kiss me again, just like you did before, only this time, I'm going to put my tongue in your mouth and I want you to use yours," I spoke, my voice falling a little deeper again in explanation.

The discomfort in my jeans was all too real but if Iris knew anything about it, she did a great job of not drawing any attention to it.

"Is that Okay?" I asked and she spoke this time.

"Yes," she replied, her breathing growing heavier from the anticipation.

I nodded as a signal for her to proceed and she lunged at me swiftly this time, her hands running through my hair as her mouth met mine. We kissed long enough for my hands to find their way to her behind and I squeezed out of necessity and longing. Once I was sure she was ready, I eased my tongue in to her mouth, gently probing to give her a feel of what it was like. She welcomed me and responded almost instantly by caressing her own tongue against mines in a playful dance sort of way. It was a little sloppy but given her inexperience was completely expected. We continued exploring and kissing and her tongue only grew more skilful and pleasurable the more practise she had. Her hands were moving of their own accord now, rubbing my neck, gripping the side of my face and clasping at my shoulders as mines trailed the base of her spine and grabbed the rim of her t-shirt. It took all of my self-control to not move them to her breasts or over her thighs to show her what she was missing out on but I respected her need for the intimacy first. A sudden moan escaped her lips right then and I knew I had to stop this before there was no turning back.

As I broke away from her I could see the longing and lust in her eyes. Both of us were out of breath and my hands were practically trembling with need. I stared at her and smiled, closing my eyes briefly before she apologised.

"Sorry, I didn't mean to make a noise," She blushed but I just shook my head.

"Noise is good, don't apologise. Trust me, guys dig that shit," I breathed, steadying my hands against her.

"Then why did you stop?" She asked curiously.

My heart jumped in response at her meek voice, her warm eyes desperate for an explanation.

"Because if I didn't, I might have taken it too far," I reasoned, the strain in my groin a reminder of the effect the girl had on me.

Iris blushed again in understanding.

"Oh," She mouthed and let out a little giggle.

I laughed too.

She peeled herself from my lap reluctantly and sat back down on the couch. With our breathing regulated and our lesson in kissing complete, I rubbed my hands against my jeans and let out a deep breath.

"So, that was..." she trailed off.

I laughed again.

"Yeah," I simply stated.

We didn't need to have a full discussion about what had just happened but I knew she was burning with questions. Not knowing if I was mentally capable of dealing with much more sexual tension I quickly sprang up from the couch and offered Iris another drink.

"No thanks, I better be going actually. I still have to get some editing done and I have an early start tomorrow," she stood too, slipping her hoodie over her head and slinging her back pack over one shoulder.

"Oh yeah? Anything exciting planned," I queried, running a hand through my hair in a bid to shake my cloudy mind.

"Nah, just some photography for the college fundraiser. My teacher roped me in to it, " She dug out her headphones from her backpack and slung them around her neck before heading towards the door.

"What about you, anything planned for tomorrow?" She smiled looking up at me with those dark eyes and played with the strap of her backpack.

"I actually have a gig tomorrow night, first one we've done in a little while locally. Hey, if you're not up to anything later on, you should totally come hang out with us before the show," I offered.

It was out before I had time to think about what I was really saying. It sounded very much like an invite to a date and that didn't bode well with me. This girl was way too nice for the likes of me. Plus, I had no intention in making this anything other than a potential hook up. Yet, I could not seem to make a clean break from her. I knew she likely deserved and perhaps even expected romance and wooing and I couldn't commit to either of those things. I almost back-peddled and removed my offer when her voice chirped;

"I'd love too!" she squealed with excitement.

'Too late' I thought to myself.

"I had a really good time tonight Dylan, thank you for inviting me over and thanks for the food," She stepped in to the lobby and turned around to face me as I held the front door open.

"And the kissing?" I teased and she instantly blushed.

It was the reaction I was hoping for.

"You'd make for a good teacher you know," She called from behind her as she walked away, my eyebrows raising with surprise again at her confident retort.

I shook my head laughing, unable to respond before closing the door and sinking back in to my couch in the now empty apartment.

Iris Steadman would be the death of me.

Chapter 11

I met with the boys down at 'The Playhouse' shortly after four pm so that we could get a little rehearsal in before tonight's show. We hadn't played a gig in over three weeks but I had no fear that we would be able to bring it just as well as we had on our short tour. Trey and Rory looked as relaxed and eager as usual, sat in animated conversation around a small wooden table beside the bar. The venue was rustic and old fashioned, with great lighting and even better acoustics. I'd never played here before but had seen a few shows to know that we were definitely still on the up and up being offered a slot to headline here. I gratefully gave each of the guys a bear hug as I approached and sat down to join in their conversation.

"What we talking about then lads," I rubbed my hands together playfully, as I arched forward, keen to see what the discussion was about.

"You, actually," Rory laughed and then gulped from his pint.

"Oh really? And what exactly were you saying about me?" I feigned hurt by placing my hand on my chest but smirked all the same.

"Oh nothing," Trey counteracted, "Just another bet," he too began laughing and the pair suddenly resembled a couple of hyena's.

"What the bloody hell are you betting about me now?" I asked incredulously.

These two were forever betting each other on the most absurd things. I'd grown used to it but sometimes their immaturity drove me crackers.

"Let me guess, I'll just have to wait and see," I rolled my eyes and they both clinked their pints together before bursting in to a fit of laughter again.

"Alright boys, I'm going to get a drink," I pushed outward from the stool and headed to the bar.

Once we'd finished our round we quickly headed out back to get our gear ready. There was one support act on before us tonight but we had agreed to loan our equipment to them to save us having to set everything back up again afterwards. We made sure everything was plugged in, tuned and the amplifiers and sound boards were stacked correctly. We placed mic stands at the appropriate points and duct tape over our proposed set list. All in all, we were our own roadies. I'd miss this if we ever made it big enough to have other people do this for us one day. I used to daydream about that a lot.

The music scene had exploded so much in the last few years that the likelihood of a band ever making it past the initial early glory stage of a few decent shows and a couple of EP's launched was staunchly slim. We had already beaten the odds by releasing a feature length album all on our own merit and our last tour had been a sell-out. We'd played to people who were passionate and sang with us and our reception had been fantastic. I only hoped we could build on that momentum and take it to the next stage.

I couldn't bear the thought of going back to my shitty desk job and answering any more pointless calls. My heart belonged to the stage and the feeling I got when I saw those faces peering up at me and mouthing every lyric. I got chills just thinking about it.

We practised a few of our tracks and settled on our final song choices for the evening. Everything sounded fine. We filtered back through to the bar to grab a couple of drinks before spending the remainder of the evening hiding out back and then thrashing around on the stage when it came our time to play.

The gig went well and the crowd seemed to enjoy our set but it wasn't a favourite show of mine. We'd played great and there was nothing in particular wrong with how the evening had panned out, it just didn't give me the same electric feel as some other shows we'd done recently. I don't know. Maybe I was overthinking things or had my expectations too high. Maybe I was a little disappointed that Iris hadn't showed or Lucy. Or any of my so called other friends for that matter. I scolded myself at how ridiculous that thought was considering I barely knew the girl I seemed infatuated with. I just knew that when I walked off the stage tonight I didn't even feel compelled to do our usual encore. There was something amiss but I couldn't put my finger on it. I guess it can't be perfect every night.

Backstage I slurped heavily on my beer bottle, having lost track of how much I'd actually drank since arriving to the venue late afternoon. I checked my phone as I always did after a gig. A text from Lucy apologising for not making the show and an invite to meet her and Reece for dinner tomorrow night. A quick thought crossed my mind of Iris but I shunned it. We hadn't even exchanged numbers so I don't know why the hell I expected to hear from her and I certainly couldn't bring myself to ring her. I sighed, leaning back against the table of drinks and scooping up another few bottles. The boys were already chilling as per usual on the provided couch and a few girls had surreptitiously made their way past the security guard and in to the vicinity, two blondes and one brunette. The latter caught my eye immediately. They smiled and giggled with each other before approaching the guys who graciously encouraged them to take a seat and share drinks. The two blonde girls sandwiched themselves between Trey and Rory snugly on the couch and the brunette sat on the arm of the chair, her gaze flitting toward me. She had a beer bottle in hand and raised it to me in a toasting gesture. Her eyes were focused and her smile slight. She had gorgeous long legs and a black short skirt with matching fitted corset. Her dark hair was splayed over one shoulder as she sipped from the cool drink, her red lipstick leaving an imprint around the rim. I gave her a friendly wink before polishing off my beer. My night would not be wasted after all it seemed. Thank god for an easy lay. Something to take my mind off things for a bit.

Chapter 12

February 2002

The following year, everything suddenly changed. That gig at 'The Playhouse' had sparked a chain of events that I never could have anticipated. The week following the gig, Trey received a call from an interested party, telling him that there was a record label now willing to sign us. When Trey broke the news, Rory screamed like a fan girl and we all barked out laughing. It's the moment we'd been working towards. Recognition and reward for working our asses off over the last five years. We were only a few months in to 2002 but I could tell it was going to be one hell of a year.

So after various meetings with the representatives from the label, the guys and I willingly signed a contract agreeing to a four album record deal. The label promised to take care of us on tour, providing us with a rider fit for a king and the chance to visit countries all over Europe. They even had a music video shoot lined up for the following month to enable us to capture a wider audience. For the first time in years, I felt fucking ecstatic. We celebrated the news with close family and friends. Lucy and Reece were there supporting me of course as my family members failed to show up. I didn't let it get me down. This news was too important in my life to be tarnished with negative energy and quite frankly I'd given up on my mother long ago. Her and her dumbass boyfriend were welcome to one another.

We were just about to embark on the first stint of our tour around the UK when a text from an unknown number grabbed my attention

"Hey stranger, hope you don't mind but I got your number from your friend Lucy. She was working at the restaurant my friends and I visited on Saturday. She told me about the deal and about you heading off on tour so I wanted to wish you well. Look me up when you get back. Iris x"

I couldn't tear the smirk from my face. I hadn't thought about Iris for a while, not since that night we'd played the gig that had brought us all the attention. I remembered my disappointment at her not showing up that night and then also how quickly it was forgotten when I'd taken that brunette home. In all honesty I'd been too busy preparing and organising for the tour to think about much else. It felt good to hear from her though and know that she also had me on her mind. I settled on replying before grabbing my seat on the bus;

"Stranger indeed! I've literally just sat on the bus right now and we're about to take off. Should be gone for around 8 weeks this time but will definitely let you know when we get back. Hope all is well with you. Take care Iris. D x"

A poke in the ribs broke me from my daydream.

"Who's caused that big cheesy grin on your face then lad?" Rory teased so I punched him in the arm.

"Mind your own business that's who," I joked before shoving my phone in my pocket.

"Plenty more of that where we're headed lads," Trey chirped in and we all looked at each other and grinned.

Who would have believed that we'd be sat in a state of the art tour bus, loaded with gadgets galore and headed for a tour over Europe. My heart burst with pride and I breathed in deep. Our journey was only beginning.

Chapter 13

Our couple of month tour flew by too quickly.

We played forty-two shows in nine different countries across Europe over eight weeks. I felt exhausted yet accomplished all the same. Our debut album had dropped halfway through the tour and our fans increased ten-fold. Radio stations were airing our single and naming us the one-to-watch over the next coming months. We sang and performed each and every single show with a tenacity and a fierceness that had been growing for quite some time. My throat was almost completely burned out from the shouting and alcohol but it felt worth every minute.

We were on our long and tedious commute back home and as the bus chugged away steadily on the all too familiar motorway, I found myself feeling anxious at the mundaneness of the on-setting sink back to reality. We'd been on a high since we'd left home and commenced our tour but the sudden realisation of it all coming to an end began weighing down on me. I'd grown used to waking up in a different city every day and seeing new faces every night. I loved dining out and living life on the road and discovering new places that I never imagined I'd be able to see. I looked wearily over at the bunks opposite me to find Rory slowly drifting off in to a seemingly peaceful slumber and Trey with his nose buried in a book. I sighed. The boys had been incredibly fun to hang out with over the course of the last few months but I knew deep down they had missed aspects of home. Don't get me wrong, they were keen to give it their all on each tour but I could sense as we were winding down the last few shows their anticipation of coming back to their own soil. I envied them. Home had no meaning for me now. Not since Dana. I couldn't deny them their excitement about seeing friends and family upon our return of course I just wouldn't be able to empathise with them about it. In fact, I was already dreading it.

In a bid to try and ease my anxiety, I began scrolling through my phone. We would be arriving home in a few short hours and I had no intention of spending the night alone. I'd had my fair share of women on the road but nothing that was of any real value. I wondered how easily I'd manage to pull tonight if I went out. Drinking was the last thing on my mind but it trumped spending a night alone in my bed and in my apartment. My phone buzzed and a text from Lucy came through.

"Can't wait to see your gorgeous face and hear all about your shenanigans. I've missed you so much. Text me when you get home! Love you."

I smiled. A genuine one. I maybe didn't have much left in the way of family these days but Lucy was always there to make up for that. Maybe I shouldn't have been so dismissive about my life here. We'd been best friends for over a decade and shared almost everything. I had missed her. I fired back a quick reply letting her know we would be home shortly and propositioning her about going out for a cheeky few later. That is if her work and Boyfriend permitted it. I dwelled on that thought, mulling over if Reece really was the right guy for Lucy just as another text came in.

"Hey stranger, remember me?"

Iris.

Shit. How could I have forgotten about her. My heart began pulsating quicker and I sat up a little straighter in the cramped bunk. I breathed out momentarily as fleeting thoughts of potential hook-ups with Iris ensued. Iris. Sweet, innocent Iris. At least that's what she implied. I felt my blood racing. Maybe coming home wasn't such a bad thing after all.

"Of course, How have you been? D "

Her reply was almost instant.

"Good. Busy, but good. I've missed you though. In fact, I haven't been able to stop thinking about you..."

I grinned.

"Is that so? Well, maybe we can do something about that... D" I replied cheekily.

"Hmmm, I like the sound of that...What do you have in mind...?"

Iris was getting rather flirty. I beamed again this time hurriedly typing my response. My excitement palpable.

"A few things...But I'd rather discuss them in person...You free tonight? D"

"Tonight?! You mean... Are you back home?!" her response clearly surprised.

"I will be...soon...Why don't you come over later? D"

I paused. Was I really doing this? Did I know what I was getting myself in to? I recalled the last time I'd spent with Iris and how aroused she'd got me with a mere kiss. The vulnerability yet willingness she'd shown had struck something in me that left me absolutely gagging for more of her. Aiding her in her sexual awakening was like a drug to me and right now I needed a fix. Something to take my depressive state back in to a distracted one. This was my ticket. My phone buzzed.

"Can be at yours for around 8...does that work for you? PS need me to bring anything...?"

"8 is fine...Yes actually, bring some food or snacks if you like since my fridge will be empty, some drinks if you can sneak some and some candles if you have any laying around. Oh, and Iris? Wear something that's easy to take off...D x"

I pressed send and then mentally slapped myself for sounding like such a horny sleaze. I couldn't help it though. I wanted to be up front about what Iris was getting in to. I'd already told her I didn't do serious relationships but I was more than willing to partake in whatever this was. The last time I had spoken to her she had confided in me about being a virgin. If this was still the case, and I believed that to be so, I needed her to mentally prepare herself for what was going to happen tonight. Losing one's virginity was a much bigger deal for a female than a male and I was not going to dick around about this, no pun intended. We were both consenting adults and I promised her I wouldn't push her. However, something in my gut told me that she had wanted this just as much as me and if that was truly the case, I was more than happy to oblige. I could be romantic when needed and although I had no intention of pursuing anything serious with Iris, I would make this night special for her as a courtesy. I wasn't a complete bastard despite what my reputation perhaps portrayed.

Chapter 14

I waved the guys off as I was the first to be dropped at home. Stood at the main door with a couple of ruck sacks and my favourite guitar slung over my shoulder, I quickly typed in the door code and headed inside. I unlocked my apartment door with my free hand and quickly entered the empty space. A quick glance around to check everything was exactly as I had left it. It was. I stooped to pick up a few letters that were piled up beneath my feet as I entered the hallway. Nothing but circulars and junk mail by the looks of it. I placed them all on the little side table at the left of the door. It was one of the few pieces of furniture I had that actually served a purpose. I placed my keys and my mobile next to the letters and dumped both bags and my guitar in a heap next to the table.

I stretched my arms above my head, yawning as I did so and then peered at the black face on my watch. It was just past six pm so I had a little time before Iris would be arriving. I decided it best to go take a shower first and foremost and then set about trying to make the apartment seem a little cosier. I didn't have much to work with but I would do my best.

Once showered, I carefully trimmed my facial hair in to a slight stubble. I wanted to make sure it looked like I'd at least put in a little bit of effort but had no intention of over-doing it. Besides, girls seemed to prefer me when I looked a little rougher. I had no idea what Iris's personal preference was when it came to such matters. With only a towel wrapped around my waist, I padded barefoot in to the bedroom in hunt of some clean clothing. I'd packed exceptionally lightly while on tour so was eternally grateful to find some oversized but comfy white cotton polo shirts and some slack fitting jeans to sink in to neatly tucked away in my chest of drawers. I didn't bother with socks or any underwear for that matter, believing both to be pretty redundant regarding my anticipated plans. A gentle douse of aftershave that Lucy had given me for Christmas and a quick once over in the mirror and I felt ready. There was a nervousness in my stomach that I didn't care to admit but I simply attributed it to the impending thought of knowing I was about to deflower Iris Steadman.

I fluffed the bed pillows and straightened out the duvet, trying to rid it of some creases. I grabbed a couple of towels from the wardrobe and laid them on top of the chest of drawers, forward thinking the likelihood that perhaps a shower would be best suited after the event. I made sure my dirty tour clothes were now neatly tucked away inside the washing hamper and my bags and guitar were shifted from the entranceway to the back bedroom. I glanced at my watch again which showed just after seven thirty and breathed out in relief at my efficiency. Everything was on track for tonight. I took a quick glance in the refrigerator, knowing I had very little left and grabbed one of the final two beers that sat cooling on the rack. My stomach welcomed the liquid but grumbled in hunger and I scolded myself for not making eating a priority. I hoped Iris would remember to bring something delectable with her.

I headed over to the docking station and plugged in my iPod. It was old and in serious need of an update but it still worked so it would do the trick. The sound of acoustic guitar strings and whiny teenage love songs roved over the apartment as I perched myself on the sofa. I took a long drag of my beer and sifted my hand through my growing locks. Reminding myself that I would need to get a hair-cut soon. I'd barely finished the bottle when the door buzzer rang. I smoothed my palms along the thighs of my jeans before I stood and headed toward the door. I breathed out and smiled, waiting patiently for her arrival.

As I swung the door open, Iris stood there gazing up at me in an almost unrecognisable demeanour. I swallowed hard.

"Fucking hell," I whispered out loud in total appreciation of the image stood before me.

Her dark hair was bundled eloquently a top her head with only a small spattering of curls falling loosely around her shoulders. Her dark eyes usually sheltered by the glasses she wore were on full show, highlighted with heavy dark eye liner and even thicker lashes. Her cheeks usually tinted pink had much more rouge in them and her lips sparkled with a clear sheen of gloss. Her neck and shoulders were openly exposed as she wore a low cut, gypsy style dress that showed off her incredible bone structure as well as hugging her womanly figure. The dress nipped in at her waist and down the curves of her hips perfectly, cutting short just above her knee. I was in awe at the transformation of the girl now gawking at me, sensing her anticipation and need for a better response than the one I had given.

"Fuck, sorry," I muttered, " Come in, please," I gestured with my arm and she smiled appreciatively as she brushed past me.

Inside the apartment she turned on her heel to look at me once more.

"Well," she giggled bashfully, spinning around to show off her new look all the while clutching on to the bag she held a little tighter, the only sign that implied she was still the same slightly shy and nervous girl that I'd met before.

"Iris, you look incredible," I beamed.

It was true. She was already gorgeous but tonight she had gone all out. I felt my heart ache in appreciation and slight disappointment. I was clearly flattered at her attempt to obviously woo me but felt the uneasiness creep in at the obvious effort she'd put in to simply spend her time indoors with me. I wasn't so sure I was worthy enough for this kind of attention. Shaking the negativity from my mind I urged her to take a seat on the couch I had been at moments earlier. She willingly obliged, seating herself delicately on the cloth sofa and swinging one gorgeously long leg over the other. She placed her bag down at her feet while tugging discreetly at the hem of her dress, evidently more self-concious at its length now she was sitting in the room with me.

I sat next to her, trying to keep as cool and as casual as possible. I'd been with a hundred girls by now. Why the fuck was I so nervous?

Iris studied me before opening her mouth, her plump lips catching my eye as they glistened in the dim lighting.

"No glasses?" I questioned, truly seeing her unobstructed full facial features for the first time.

"Contacts," She breathed, a little grin toying at the side of her mouth.

"You look great too Dylan, truly," She began, her eyes roaming over me then, taking in the full picture.

"You've lost weight though?" She queried.

I shrugged, "Maybe a little," I spoke with ease.

She was right. It most certainly wasn't intentional but the hectic tour life meant food wasn't regularly scheduled and as such, it had physically taken its toll. That and the fact I had given my everything on stage every night for the last few months.

"Didn't they feed you while you were gone?!" She teased and I laughed.

She hadn't lost her sense of humour.

"Just beer mostly," I joked and she giggled too.

"Maybe I can fix that?" She spoke, her hand delving in to the bag at the base of the couch.

She pulled out a small black tray and offered it to me. I looked at her quizzically, taking the box from her and opening it with sudden interest. Inside, nine strawberries were delicately covered with chocolate. Three white, three milk, three dark. I gazed back at her with an arched eyebrow. She blushed.

"I thought you might be hungry," She replied sheepishly, pulling at the dress hem again as she unfolded her leg and placed both feet flat to the ground, her knees tightly pinned together.

"You guessed right," I remarked, studying her as opposed to the delicious fruit now at my fingertips.

Her cheeks deepened in colour, a clear indication that she got my meaning.

"Shall I?" I coaxed, picking up one of the strawberries and drawing it closer to my mouth. Her eyes lit up in eager anticipation as she watched me take a bite. I kept eye contact with her the entire time.

"Mmm. So good. Here, " I grabbed another from the box and leaned toward her.

Placing the fruit as close to her mouth as possible before she carefully parted her lips and took a bite of the delicious snack. I waited for her to finish before prompting her.

"Well?" I grinned.

She smiled.

"So good," she repeated and we laughed.

Things were clearly off to a good start. I could sense a little apprehension on her part but I pinned that down to her nervousness. She held herself well though and was even bold enough to make the first move. I took it upon myself to take charge then, and coax her out of her shell. There was a sexy as hell women lurking beneath this girl and I was desperate to unearth her.

"Any other surprises in that bag of yours?" I nudged her playfully before wolfing down another strawberry.
They really were tasty and I was most definitely in need of some real food.

She gave a little smirk before reaching in and pulling out a tall, glass bottle. Some sort of wine or champagne, I couldn't be sure. She laid it on the table and proceeded to pull out another few items. A glass jar with what appeared to be various nuts and candied fruit inside, a small rectangular box with around six candles, another small box that was pink and black on the outside but I had no idea what it contained and finally a piece of cloth material that looked a lot like a blindfold. She visibly gulped a little before looking back at me.

"I wasn't exactly sure what all you meant when you texted me, so I hope this is ok," She seemed incredibly nervous now, almost embarrassed in fact so I took this as my chance to put her mind at ease.

"That is EXACTLY what I had in mind when I texted you," I stated, running my hands over the various items.

She breathed outward in almost relief.

"I'll tell you what, why don't you make yourself comfy. Relax, I'll get a couple of glasses, you can open that bottle and pour us a few drinks while I make a last few minute arrangements," I offered.

She nodded perching herself forward to the utmost edge of the couch.

Her actions only highlighted her eagerness and her apprehension. She was keen and willing but understandably nervous. I would make it my mission tonight to ensure that she felt different before she left.

Chapter 15

I went to the kitchen firstly in the hunt for two wine glasses that were hidden in the back of one of my crockery cupboards. I rarely had people over here but from time to time Lucy and I had enjoyed the odd glass of bubbly to celebrate an occasion such as a birthday or Christmas. I gave them a once over with my dish towel before proceeding back to the living room. I set the glasses down on the coffee table and swiftly scooped up the other items.

"Be back in a minute," I winked at her before heading off in the direction of my bedroom.

Once inside, I quickly drew the curtains and laid the items on the bed. I set about unboxing the scented candles and placed a few around the room. I carefully lit them with the matches I kept inside my underwear drawer. It was my back up place for a light should I run out of fuel on my zippo. I briefly contemplated going for a quick smoke then but cast it away out of respect for Iris. I didn't want the smell of stale smoke to ruin the moment. God, I couldn't believe how much I was over thinking this. I also couldn't ever recall being handed the opportunity to partake in something quite as special as this. I felt honoured to have been chosen. I know how cocky that must sound but my entire life I was accustomed to being treated like the riff raff or the driftwood. I'd had girlfriends sure, but they'd been around the block more than I cared to ever imagine and had shown very little interest in pleasing me. It was always about them. I wanted to make tonight about Iris because subconsciously I think I knew that she wanted to please me in return. Maybe I was being narcissistic. Maybe I was yielding this entire evening to my advantage. Or maybe, just maybe this was something...more.

I took the jar of sweet and savoury goodies from the bed and left it on the side table, knowing they would make for a good after sex snack if it got that far. I peered at the remaining two items. One was indeed a soft, silk eye mask that was clearly intended to be used as a blindfold. I laughed inwardly to myself at Iris's not so subtle hint of how she foresaw her evening panning out and my inner ego growled with pride. The last box, on closer inspection contained a small plastic bottle with raspberry flavoured lubricant. My eyebrows raised with pleasant surprise. Was this for her pleasure or mine? Maybe Iris wasn't so innocent after all? I placed the bottle on the nightstand too, hooking the blindfold just over the corner of the bedframe. I took one final glance around the room, happy with the setting before I made my way back toward Iris in the sitting room.

She was happily sipping from her glass as I entered the room. Her eyes bright and alive. Her body language was easing up and her high heeled shoes were now placed beside her bag.

"Here," She stretched out her arm, offering the secondary glass to me to which I gladly accepted.

I took a swig from the flute, enjoying the feel of the liquid in my mouth before swallowing. I smiled at Iris and then sat next to her as before.

"So how was the tour," She turned her frame toward me, angling herself on the couch so that one of her legs was now tucked up beneath her.

She looked comfortable yet sophisticated and much more mature than the last time I'd met with her. That night felt like a lifetime ago.

"Honestly, it was incredible," I beamed, my heart still reeling from our success.

"I can't even begin to imagine. The radio has been playing you guys non-stop. It's so surreal!" She squealed, her inner fan girl apparent.

Another ego stroke. My chest tightened.

"I know, it's a little insane for sure," I agreed.

I sipped hard again, this time nearly emptying my glass.

"What about you, what have you been up to since we saw each other last?" I ushered her to respond.

She grabbed the bottle from the coffee table to top up my glass respectfully and then proceeded to fill her own to the brim.

"A bit manic too if I'm honest," She sighed. "I've been inundated with job offers since completing my college project so I've had to work hard on various portfolio's for job interviews. It's so good to be noticed but taking pictures now has become a full time job all by itself. There's a lot of work involved," she motioned and drank gracefully again from her glass.

I nodded in agreement.

I was happy for Iris, truly. She had showcased real potential so it was only right that she should be exploring career opportunities based on her talent. Her eye for detail would catapult her in the direction of a serious career should she choose that path. It was always humbling to hear someone following their passion.

"Iris that's incredible. I'm proud of you, you should be too," I urged.

She shrugged, almost shrinking her credibility. I wanted to banish her negative thoughts and empower her to realise her full potential.

"Here's to following our passion," I clinked my glass with hers in a celebratory manner.

"To passion," she breathed, her eyes growing wild with ulterior thoughts.

"Speaking of..." I placed my now empty glass on the table and picked up another strawberry.

"Why don't we pick up where we left off?" I took a small bite of the strawberry this time before raising it up towards Iris' lips.

She opened willingly but instead of biting down, she sucked on the tip of the strawberry, the soft milk chocolate oozing in to her mouth.

She grinned at me then and my cock went hard.

I placed my arm around the back of the couch and leaned toward her. My lips quickly finding hers as my other hand softly grasped the edge of her cheek. Our lips danced momentarily and my tongue lapped at the chocolate remnants as she welcomed me eagerly. With our eyes closed and our mouths entwined we picked up the pace. She tasted as sweet as the fruit we'd been consuming and I could have sworn she'd had some serious practise since the last time we'd kissed. I tried to discard the thought, focusing instead on her eagerness and willingness to succumb to my need. Her new confidence clearly teetering her to be bolder as she grabbed the collar of my polo shirt with both hands almost aggressively in a bid to bring me even closer to her.

I groaned from both surprise and sheer want as my hands now lingered over the fine material covering her breasts. I palmed them both equally as the kiss deepened, earning me a soft mewling sound in response. I smiled to myself, unable to deny the powerful effect this was having on my ego. She tilted her head back then, eyes squeezed shut as her hands roved through my hair before she guided my head to her chest. My cock throbbed at her need to show me what she wanted, after all who doesn't love a woman in charge? I heeded her wishes and expertly freed her left breast from the dress with ease, kissing down her clavicle and softly swirling my tongue around the exposed nipple. I watched and licked as it hardened beneath my mouth, sucking on it sweetly as she moaned again. I could practically feel her body melting beneath my touch so I continued my onslaught. I freed the right breast now, repeating the same motion as I had done with the other, gently licking and then sucking the flesh until her body began arching inwardly toward me. I peered up at her face then and revelled in the look in her eyes as she watched me, her cheeks flushed, her mouth wide and her eyes glossing over. I had to get things moving and fast or I was never going to be able to last.

"Maybe we should take this to the bedroom," my husky voice breathed and she nodded.

Her breathing was already becoming rigid as was the growing restriction in my jeans. I carefully held her hand in mine to escort her from the couch and in to the bedroom.

Inside, the dim lighting from the candles gave an effervescent glow around the room and her eyes beamed with pleasant delight.

I turned to face her then, both her palms in my own and spoke,

"You sure you want to do this?" I asked seriously.

I was a man of my word. If she wanted to back out she could have at any minute. Yes, my dick wouldn't be charmed but I was not going to push her in to anything she wasn't comfortable with.

"I want this," She breathed. "I want it to be you".

My heart beat quickened and my arms wrapped around her then.

I nuzzled in to her neck kissing her and nipping her from behind her ear and all the way down to her exposed breasts. Another couple of teasing kisses before I spoke again.

"Good. Now, lay down on the bed," I commanded.

She nodded again, her nervousness shielded by her impending lust. She sat on the edge of the bed and gently pushed herself back towards the headboard. Her eyes gazing up at me expectantly so I began to strip. I rid myself of my shirt in one swift motion and then peeled myself from my jeans. My erection protruded toward her and I watched her eyes glaze over with seeming pleasure and curiosity. I wondered if she'd ever physically seen a man naked before. I crept toward her, mindful of where she lay and knelt on the end of the bed.

"Pull up your dress," I spoke, my voice deep.

Her hands carefully made their way to her thighs and she tugged at the material so that it now hung up past her hips and around her navel. Her luscious breasts spilling over the top still from where I'd released them earlier and her black panties now on show.

"Good," I grinned.

It was an enchanting view.

I watched her chest rise and fall as I leaned down to grab one of her legs in my hands, her eyes never leaving me as I began kissing her softly at the inner ankle. I held her leg momentarily as I worked a trail of hot wet kisses up one of her calves and then settled on her inner thigh. Her breathing growing more rapid the higher I kissed. My mouth made its way to the apex of her thighs now, and I paused to take her in. This gorgeous girl strewn across my bed, beneath me and wanting me it seemed as much as I wanted her. My aching hard on pressed deeply in to the bed then as my mouth breathed over the thin black material of her knickers.

She moaned then, her head shooting back against the pillows as desire swept over her.

I had her where I wanted her. But it wasn't enough.

I peeled myself back from her, the motion making her eyes shoot open and her stare at me incredulously.

"Take it off," I barked.

She squinted at me, puzzled.

She shimmied the dress over her head and threw it to the floor.

I arched an expectant eyebrow at her, and pointed teasingly at the fine lace underwear that hid her modesty.

"All of it," I scoffed.

She grinned then, in understanding and quickly peeled the material from her flesh before discarding it to the side.

"There," I beamed.

Iris lay there fully nude as my eyes took in her womanly figure. Her voluptuous hips and breasts did not disappoint and the soft mound between her thighs looked every inch as delectable as her entire body did. Her hands were nervously pinned by her sides as though she didn't know what to do with them so I quickly stepped in to action.

"Do you trust me?" I asked breathily and she nodded.

"Of course," She mouthed, her eyes searching for what was about to happen next.

I grabbed the blindfold from the edge of the bed and leaned above her, my generous cock grazing teasingly against her thigh. She shivered beneath me.

"Close your eyes," I spoke softly.

She obeyed without hesitation. I carefully lifted her head for a moment with one hand and slung the blindfold over her eyes with the other. I wanted her to fully concentrate on the sensations and depriving her of one sense was bound to awaken the others. I kissed her soft mouth with a passion intended for the most daring romantic. It had the desired effect as her body arched toward me of its own will. I ran my mouth along her jawline, between her breasts this time and licked and teased my tongue across her sternum and above her navel. She arched again, this time I pinned her hips down against the bed.

"Relax," I breathed and she remained still.

I kissed and lapped the area between her thighs feeling her tense beneath me. Her short burst moans grew longer and louder as I proceeded, delving deeper and savouring her delicious taste. I paid careful attention to her clitoris, to give her maximum pleasure but I knew she wouldn't be able to last long before climaxing if I kept at this pace. I trailed my index finger up her right inner thigh, softly sweeping the delicate flesh there for a while as I continued to lick her out. Once I was sure she was ready, I carefully placed the tip of one finger at her entrance, prodding gently. She immediately tensed so I urged her to relax once more. I slid my finger in gently to give her time to adjust to the new sensation. She sighed as I began to enter and exit her with my finger all the while simultaneously stimulating her with my tongue. Her breathing ragged and her hands now entangled in my hair gave me the prompt I needed to slide another one inside her and I did so, this time with ease. I knew she was close when she began moaning my name. My cock throbbed in response, desperate for attention. 'All in good time' I told myself. With three fingers inside her and my tongue darting over her she was soon spent. Her body tightening around my fingers and her hands clasping the back of my neck as she came. It went as perfectly as I had imagined.

Sighing contently, she tore the mask from her eyes. Her cheeks fully flushed now and her eyes gleaming. She picked herself up a little from the bed and stared down at me.

"That was, fucking amazing," she cursed and I couldn't help the laugh that escaped my lips.

"Good, I'm glad you enjoyed it," I winked at her, my own cheeky smile in place.

"Is it my turn now?" She asked suddenly and my balls tightened.

"You don't have to if you don-" she cut me off.

"I want to. I want to taste you," She mouthed as she crept toward me.

Her dark eyes were now hungrily taking in my body and I had little willpower to stop her. The previous activity had left me reeling for touch and I was not about to turn down an opportunity like this with such a willing participant.

"You wanna be in charge?" I teased and she nodded enthusiastically.

"Very well," I grinned, laying on my back across the bed so that she had full control over what happened next.

I watched her curiously as she eyeballed my raging cock. I wasn't at all sure how confident she would be but I was happy to play along for now. She quickly grabbed the blindfold in a bid to cover my eyes but I grabbed her wrist to refrain her.

"You know, I get more turned on if I can actually SEE what's happening," I looked her dead in the eye.

It was true. Men had a much more visceral need for visual stimulation than women. I envied them somewhat for that.

"Okay," she placed the material down but quickly snapped up the little bottle of lube from the bedside.

She waved the bottle at me teasingly and said "Any objections?" and I shook my head amused.

Fuck.

The suspense was driving me crazy.

I looked on as she carefully applied the cool liquid in to the palm of her hand. She came closer to me, positioning her body between my thighs before grasping the base of my dick. I tensed at the sudden contact and relished in the feel of the slick and sliding feeling as her hand rubbed me from the base to the tip. Her fingers held on a little tighter than I was used to but again, I decided to go with it. This was new for her after all and who was I to discourage someone so willing to learn. She kept up her rhythmic strokes for a good five minutes before her eyes began to wonder. She had a look in them that told me she was keen to try something else so I prepared myself mentally for what was about to happen next.

She removed her hand from the shaft of my penis and placed both palms on my hips. I looked at her, her eyes graciously gazing over my erect cock before her mouth presented itself. I moaned at the feeling of warmth as she engulfed me. Her tongue flicked the underside of my dick as she bobbed her head up and down, sucking on my hardened flesh. My eyes shut momentarily, basking in the feel of her mouth around me. She may have been inexperienced but by fuck she knew how to master the blowjob. One of her hands left my thigh and her fingers began fondling my balls as she continued to suck me off. I don't know how in the hell she knew what to do but if she kept this up there was no way I was going to last much longer. I fought hard against the overwhelming sensation to come right then and release my seed between her juicy lips. It was time to take it further. I hooked my finger under her chin, catching her attention and pleading with her to look at me.

She stopped sucking then and her mouth made a 'pop' sound as she released my dick from her grasp. I growled inwardly at the sudden loss of contact and flipped her beneath me. She squealed then, giddy with excitement.

I quickly leaned to the deskside drawer and removed the small foil wrapper. I peeled the pack open, rolling the condom over my dick carefully looking at Iris the entire time. Once ready, I positioned myself just above her.

"The key to this is just to relax. Can you do that for me Iris?" My voice serious and wanting.

Her chocolate brown eyes came alive once more and she nodded.

"Anything," she practically begged.

I stiffened.

I rubbed between her legs once more with my free hand and used the other hand for support before placing my dick at her entrance. I eased my way in to her opening feeling her entire frame tighten beneath me. It took a lot of will power to do this as slowly as she needed. My cock was desperate for more. Once inside, I gave her another moment to adjust before withdrawing and repeating the action. I did this a few times to make things a little easier for her. The restraint was making me even more excited. On about the fifth attempt, her mouth opened and a little moan erupted. I took this as my cue to pick up the pace and stay inside her. I would be gentle but I'd also make it count. Her hands gripped my shoulders at first then wrapped their way to my lower back as I pushed in and out of her. Her hips moved freely and tried in vain to match my thrusts. I continued kissing and sucking on her breasts which warranted me even more lustful moans and I knew she was actually enjoying this. That thought was enough to push me to the edge. I thrust faster this time but still carefully as I didn't want her hurting too much the morning after. I kept a steady rhythm and when I was almost there, I began thumbing her clitoris. She cried out, her head lolling back and her mouth screaming my name then. A few more sharp thrusts and I came too.

The deed was done. I had de-flowered Iris Steadman. My inner ego rejoiced.

Chapter 16

The following evening Lucy and I had agreed to meet for drinks so that we could catch up and reminisce. I'd truly missed her while on tour and I wanted to check in on her to see how things were going with her boyfriend Reece. They'd been together for just over a year now and although Lucy wasn't incredibly smart when it came to choosing men, I couldn't fault Reece. The very few times we'd met he seemed like a stand-up guy. He was clearly smitten with her and I hoped it would remain that way. No one deserved happiness more than Lucy. Truly, she was the sweetest, most hardworking and reliable girl I knew.

I was just entering the pub when my text alert sounded.

"Can't stop thinking about last night...and you..." .

I grinned. Me neither.

I was just about to head to the bar when I caught sight of a flailing arm at the back end of the dimly lit pub. Lucy. My grin only intensified. I made my way over to the table where she sat and smiled. Lucy jumped from her seat and slung her arms around me.

"Gah, I've missed you!" She squealed.

I'd missed her too.

It'd been far too long since our last catch up.

"Where's Reece?" I glanced at the empty table.

"A work thing," she groaned.

Not good.

"Things okay with you guys?" I asked wearily, not sure I was ready to hear the answer.

We both took our seats then.

"Yeah, yeah everything's fine. We just don't see enough of one another. Between my shifts at the restaurant and his late ours in the office. Adult life sucks!" She bellowed and I chuckled.

"That it does," I agreed.

"Hold on though," she began, a massive smirk on her lips, "What were you smiling at when you came in?" She pressed.

Lucy. Doesn't miss a fucking trick.

I shook my head nervously and laughed.

"Dylan Wakefield, are you keeping secrets from me?" She teased.

"Impossible!" I retorted.

"Is that her name?" She joked and I burst out laughing.

"Not anymore," I replied jokingly and then cringed at how crude my statement was.

Lucy laughed and shook her head.

"Ooooo Dylan got some action!" She jeered. "Who's the lucky lady and when can I meet her?"

I smiled whole-heartedly at my best friend and my mind foolishly cast back to Lucy's sweet sixteen birthday party.

It was 1999 and Lucy had invited me and a few of my so called 'friends' over tonight to celebrate her turning sixteen. I was initially very much against the idea, knowing fine well the house would be laden with annoying popular kids and a bunch of underage girls but I didn't have the heart to break it to Lucy. She had made me promise to show face and I was not about to let her down. My little Lucy wanted me there so I would be there.

The front door was already ajar by the time we rolled up. Me and two of the lads that I jammed with had a few joints and some pints before we headed over. I was grateful to have taken the edge off a little in preparation for this. Taking a deep breath, I lead the way for me and the guys as we bustled past a throng of teenage bodies inside the lobby. My eyes frantically scanned the premises, searching for my special lady. A loud cheer erupted to my left so I whipped my head around quickly to catch the sight. Lucy slammed an empty shot glass on the table and raised her hands in victory as a group of lads and girls cheered her on. I frowned. An uneasiness crept over me, then a stark realisation. Lucy wasn't so little any more. Her gorgeous dark hair had its signature loose curls flowing around her like a brunette halo. She was wearing a pastel pink strapless dress that nipped in at the waist and kicked out a little at her hips. It suited her perfectly. Her eyes found mine then, my head awash with thoughts of her throughout the years I'd known her. Her face lit up at my presence and she quickly shoved her way through the crowd to meet me. I urged the guys to go find us some drinks in a bid to have the moment alone with her. They got the hint and soon wandered off in the direction of the kitchen.

I turned back around to find Lucy stood before me, an absolute image of perfection even though I knew no such sanctity truly existed. She came close though.

"You made it!" She beamed as she threw her slender arms around me.

She felt warm and smelled like wild flowers and coconut. I gripped her a little tighter and held her just a little bit longer. Something about tonight had me worried that I was about to lose her.

"Wouldn't miss it for the world," I smiled at her.

She crinkled up her face knowingly and playfully smacked me on the arm.

"You scrub up good!" She stroked the lapel of my black button down shirt approvingly.

When I wasn't working and wearing that stupid ass uniform I wore my torn jeans, black band tee-shirts and my battered converse. Tonight I'd gone for a pair of fitted black denims with a matching black shirt and a pair of black vans slip on's. I felt a little dressed up but not overly so and I was secretly grateful that my effort hadn't gone unmissed. Lucy never missed a trick.

"Thanks babe, wanted to fit in you know?" I joked and her laughter pierced my soul.

"You, fit in?" She teased and I nudged her back.

Fuck. Life always seemed so fucking easy around her. Why couldn't it always be like that?

"Anyways," I reached in to my back pocket and produced a small gift box.

"Sorry it isn't much," I shrugged before handing her the wrapped gift.

"Dylan! You didn't need to do that for me, I said no gifts!" She whined but there was no way I was going to come here empty handed.

Besides, it was a mere trinket. Just something I wanted her to have that would somehow always remind her of me. No matter what happened. I prayed she'd never forget.

She carefully peeled off the paper and I watched her, mesmerised by her expressions as she eagerly opened the box.

Inside was a thin silver chain and attached to it a metallic guitar pick. It had the phrase 'Some-day' inscribed on it. A reminder of our promise to each other over the last eight years that we were going to get out of here and do something with our lives. We were going to make it. I wanted to believe it but I never truly did. She did believe in it though and that's what counted. Some day.

Her hand wiped away a stray tear from her cheek and she grinned. She had no words and I had no desire to hear any. I simply smiled back at her knowingly and threw my arm around her once more. No matter where life would take us we would always have these kinds of memories, a reel of all the moments we simply 'got' one another without speech. There wasn't another human being on the entire planet that I could have felt so connected with other than her. My Lucy. I still didn't deserve her.

We broke free moments later and I watched as she quickly swiped at her cheeks delicately before exhaling.

"Right," she breathed, "I think I need another drink!" she laughed and I nodded.

"Go on ahead, I'll catch up with you in a bit," I offered.

She gave me her biggest smile, stretched up on her toes to peck me sweetly on the cheek before being carted off by a bunch of her friends in the direction of a nearby keg.

I smoothed my now sweating palms on the thighs of my jeans before setting off on my own drink hunt. But first, I needed a smoke.

Once the party was in full swing, I found myself a comfy spot in one of the couches in the dining area. Lucy's parent's house wasn't overly big but it had a great open plan layout which made everywhere seem more spacious. More and more people had arrived over the duration of the evening. The lads I'd arrived with had bailed over an hour ago but I wasn't quite ready to depart yet.

"Mind if we sit here bud?" A tall, red headed guy asked, a beer bottle in each hand.

"Nah man, not at all," I gestured to the free space next to me.

The red headed guy and his short friend quickly plunked themselves down and visibly relaxed. They sipped from their beers and muttered their thanks. I raised my half empty cup in a salute.

"You guys friends with Lucy?" I asked, curiosity getting the better of me.

Most of the people I recognised from Lucy's year at school or people she had described in her life during some of our frequent conversations. I was having a hard time trying to place the two currently sat beside me. They looked about my age.

"Is that the girl who lives here?" The short one answered, half cut.

"Uhh, yeah," I snickered.

"Sorry man, no we don't actually know her. My mate Rory here followed an invite from his fuck buddy to join her here and dragged me with him. He still hasn't found her though," The tall one stated before shaking his head and grinning.

Rory groaned and then chugged from his bottle.

"I see," I sipped again from my cup unsure how to feel about that statement.

"It's cool man, they do this thing often. Oh and she's the same age as us by the way in case you were wondering," the tall one quickly explained seemingly sensing my apprehension.

I nodded.

"I'm Trey," he extended his hand courteously and I shook it back politely.

"Dylan,".

"Cool name! Like Bob?" he asked intrigued and I just grinned.

"I guess yeah," I smiled.

"So you're into music?" Trey prompted.

Rory's attention waned from our conversation as his eyes followed the girls that would pass by.

"Sort of, yeah," I replied modestly.

"Cool, you play?" Trey asked.

"Guitar," I replied bluntly.

"Nice! I play bass, Rory plays drums. We've been looking for a guitarist for a while now but no one ever seems to commit. It's hard going trying to find other folks willing to go for it these days," Trey sipped coolly from one of his two bottles after he spoke.

I nodded.

Interesting.

"You guys play a lot?" I queried, genuinely intrigued.

"Sure! We rehearse most days. Had a few gigs in the past too. Just a shame we can't find the right front man. People are so fucking fickle you know?" He stated and I laughed.

"I hear you dude".

"Hey, we should totally jam some time!" Trey offered and Rory's gaze drifted back in to our conversation.

"Fuck yeah! We should jam sometime," Rory added, clearly feeling the effects of his drink.

I smiled at the pair.

There was something charming about them.

Fuck it. Couldn't hurt to try out with someone else for a change. Besides, our band were going nowhere. The guys were too busy getting smashed, laid or stoned to even give two flying fucks about a career in music. I needed a break. A breath of fresh air if you will.

I liked Trey. He had passion. The same kind I felt when I thought about music. It was evident from the moment I'd mentioned my name.

Rory...I wasn't quite sure what to make of yet.

"Sounds good. Time and place lads and I'll be there," I motioned my cup towards Trey and he clinked it with his bottle.

And that was how I came to meet Trey and Rory. Funny how things pan out.

We drank and conversed and the hours suddenly seemed to fly by. The house had grown a little quieter but there were still groups of people and music playing. I'd caught sight of a guy leaned against the kitchen counter, deep in conversation with Lucy. I didn't want to admit it but I'd been watching her from a distance the entire night. This guy had been relentless in his pursuit of conversing with her and he had now succeeded it seemed. Lucy was smiling and laughing and clearly flattered by whatever patter he was spinning for her. She flicked her hair often and leaned in to touch him flirtatiously. I kept trying to look else-where but I was drawn to it. A few moments later, he held her hand and guided her towards the stairs. My fist automatically clenched a little tighter in response knowing exactly where he was leading her. Fuck.

I swallowed my protective instinct hard and offered the guys another drink. I found a half full bottle of rum on a nearby table and started pouring shots into a couple of plastic cups. Trey and Rory drank their shots with ease as did I. I tried to rid my mind of the worry currently running through it. Once the bottle was gone, Rory went and fetched a case of beer from the fridge. A few empty bottles later and the drink had really taken its toll. Rory was practically passed out on the couch, his eyes closing every few seconds and Trey was slurring his words. I could feel my head begin to spin too but I refused to give in. Not yet. I was just about to grab another bottle when the guy from earlier stumbled down the stairs. He had the dirtiest fucking grin on his face and started high-fiving a bunch of ass-holes as he re-entered the living room. My stomach churned with contempt.

I looked impatiently at the stairs, waiting for Lucy to follow suit but she never did. The same uneasiness I'd felt earlier while watching her knock back shots slowly crept over me. Something was wrong. The guy who'd come downstairs and a bunch of his mates made for the front door, spilling out in to the street in their drunken stupor and seemingly calling it a night. Trey's voice broke my train of thought momentarily.

"Hey dude, we're gonna head now. Think I need to get Rory home before he crashes for good," he laughed.

"Yeah man, it was fucking awesome to meet you both," I shook Trey's hand respectfully.

"You've got my number now though so give me a text later in the week and we can arrange a jam session yeah?" Trey offered and I nodded.

"Of course, can't wait," I replied truthfully.

But right now my mind was on other things.

I helped Trey in escorting Rory to their Taxi outside and then quickly ran upstairs. There were only a few people remaining but most of them were either passed out or close to sleeping. I found Lucy's bedroom door and knocked gently.

"Don't come in here," her voice bellowed over the music.

I heard her sniffle.

"Lucy?" I breathed as I turned the handle.

I could see her about to snap at the door being opened until she caught my face.

"You're still here," She cried, and her face broke then.

My blood instantly began to boil red hot. I was going to fucking kill that guy.

I closed the door behind me and walked slowly over to where she sat on the bed. Her hair dishevelled and her cheeks mascara stained. Her hands were covering her mouth and her soft cries had her body trembling. I sat next to her and wrapped my arms around her. I took a deep breath trying to compose myself. I fucking knew this would happen.

I listened intently and sympathetically as Lucy relayed the story about the guy who'd just left and how he'd taken her virginity. My worst fear had been confirmed. I'd always suspected Lucy had maintained her innocence but had never pressed her on the matter. It was much more personal for girls and I respected that I may not be the person she'd want to confide in about something like that. I watched helplessly as she sat there balling her eyes out in embarrassment because she'd said the experience had been such a disappointing one. Yes, she'd been willing but the prick had left her only moments after the deed, spouting nonsense about not wanting anything serious and trying to convince her he'd had a 'good time'. She broke down again in the re-telling of it all and it pained me to see her this cut up about a fucking asshole. Men were fucking cunts. Truly.

She deserved so much better. I wanted to rip his fucking head off. He'd been granted an opportunity that most guys would die for yet he showed no respect and left Lucy feeling worthless. I gritted my teeth.

A few teary moments later, she'd finally composed herself enough to pick her head up from my shoulder and look at me.

"How was your night?" She asked and I couldn't help but smile.

"Fuck sake Lucy, it was your birthday. Nobody gives a shit about what I've been up to tonight," I laughed and she shook her head.

"Not true," She grinned, "I do," and she smiled.

It was that heartbreakingly beautiful smile that was so selfless and so sincere that it cut right through me. I wanted to tell her that she was the only reason I came but I knew deep down that she already knew that. I wanted to tell her about meeting Trey and Rory but somehow it all seemed so insignificant in comparison to what she had just relayed to me. I wanted to offer to kill the son of a bitch who'd broken her heart but I knew that would only upset her more. So instead, I remained silent. Silent on the matters that cut too close to the heart because frankly, I felt moments from losing it myself.

"Get some sleep babe, you're exhausted," I kissed her forehead.

She yawned then and we both smiled.

I stood up from the bed but she tugged at my hand.

"Dylan, can you stay with me? Just for tonight? I just don't want to be alone right now," she muttered drowsily.

The panging sensation clutched at my chest again.

"Of course. Anything for you my love. Scoot over," I ushered her to lay down in bed and crawled in beside her.

My arms protectively wrapping themselves around her and spooning her just like we did as kids. She quickly relaxed against me and I did my best to keep my composure. Before long, my own eyes grew heavy and I soon drifted off in to a conflicted yet peaceful sleep with the scent of Lucy's coconut shampoo warming my heart.

Chapter 17

I never did confess to her how much that night had pained me. Her innocence being stripped away from her in a reckless moment with a practical stranger. It ached something awful in my gut. I knew I would never be able to save her from all of the mistakes she would make over the course of her life but I was willing to try. I hated that waste of space for being able to have his hands on her in ways I could only dream and yet I knew my thoughts were perverse. Lucy and I were friends, nothing more.

I also never told Lucy that the following night I tracked him down with a group of his mates at one of the local skate parks. I made sure he wouldn't forget my face. Especially since I'd pounded his so easily. His so called friends had done a runner after I threw the first punch, clearly terrified at my manic outburst. I made sure he paid for the way he'd treated my Lucy. I also made sure he would never tell her what went down that day.

I looked at Lucy's arm waving in front of my face.

"Earth to Dylan, where'd you go buddy?" She teased, shaking me from my trance.

"Sorry babe, just reminiscing that's all," I reassured her, her gesture snapping me back from my trip down memory lane.

"Really? About last night and this new girl?" She egged me on.
Lucy fucking Barron.

My Lucy. Sat before me all grown up and all woman. She was all sweetness and light mostly and I adored her. We couldn't be much more opposite if we tried. I tried not to dwell on that fact but from time to time my mind wandered how the hell she had put up with me and our friendship for as long as she had. I was grateful of course. Some days I only get by because of her. I don't know where I'd have been if it weren't for her warm spirit and those kind eyes.

Eyes that were now solely focused on me as my mind wandered again.

"Dylan!" She snapped her fingers in front of my face.

"Fuck," I blinked. "Sorry," I muttered another apology.

"What the hell are you thinking about now?" She groaned and I laughed.

"You, actually," I teased.

She squinted at me, her cute frown trying to gauge the situation.

"Do I wanna know?" She queried before a grin broke across that sweet face of hers.

I shook my head and laughed.

"Anyways, you were saying?" I motioned for the waitress to get us another couple of drinks.

"I believe you were about to tell me about the girl who has you all screwed up in the head already," she pressed her index finger against the side of my skull to emphasise her point.

I shook my head and laughed.

"Is it that obvious?" I raised a single eyebrow and met her eyes.

Lucy was oblivious to just how true her words were. That and the fact that the statement could be applied to two women in my life. One of them being her.

"You've literally had that shit-eating grin on your face non-stop and I can't seem to get your full attention for longer than a second. Yes, it's obvious," she smiles at me, her curiosity lurking.

I decide to confide in her, just as I always do. I leave out one important detail though in my retelling of events. I fail to mention that Iris was a virgin before I had my way with her. For some reason, I feel uncomfortable sharing that fact with Lucy. I'm not entirely sure why.

"God, Dylan. You sound smitten," she gushes and I give her my signature wink.

"She's pretty great," I reply truthfully before taking a huge swallow of my pint.

"It's about time someone tried to tame that wild spirit of yours," Lucy sipped on her jack, welcoming the cool liquid.

"I thought that was your job?" I mocked and she nudged my shin beneath the table with her converse shoe.

"I'm so pleased for you Dylan. You seem so happy".

And I was.

For the first time in a long time. Everything seemed to be falling in to place. The band were harbouring some successes, my best friend was in a seemingly healthy and potentially serious relationship and I had Iris to concentrate on. My life didn't feel bleak or meaningless any more. It had purpose. I raised my glass and clinked it respectively with Lucy's one.

"Now," she grinned. "Tell me all about the tour," her eyes concentrating on my features.

And so I spent the next few hours sharing stories and laughing with my best friend.

Maybe coming home wasn't such a bad thing after all.

FIFTEEN YEARS LATER

Chapter 18

September 2016

No words could truly capture or describe the complete and utter devastation that tore through my body at the accusation. My heart sank to the pit of my stomach and bile rose in my throat. My hands trembled with sickening rage and my head pounded from the sound of my pulse vibrating in my ear drums. How the fuck had it come to this? Right on the brink of a prestigious career finish and a stellar final album release and suddenly I'd been thrown to the wolves. The press were having a field day, the record label had gone ape-shit, threatening to drop us and trying to re-negotiate their way out of already signed contracts and the boys were heavily encouraging me to lawyer-up. What the fuck. I stood motionless as the statement continued to air out on live TV.

"Iris Steadman, now thirty years old, has courageously come forward in the wake of the 'hashtag me too' campaign to bravely share her story. Steadman has said she was only fifteen years of age when she was groomed and harassed by front man 'Dylan Wakefield' now thirty-six who was believed to be around twenty-one at the time. 'Wakefield' the lead singer and guitarist with the band, "The Attachment theory" is currently on tour and is yet to make an official statement. In a report issued to the police by Steadman, it is believed that Mr Wakefield 'grossly manipulated' his position in order to have sexual relations with the under-ager during an on-off relationship between the pair that she said lasted for 'around three years' in early 2001, right at the wake of the singer's rise to stardom. More information to follow after this short break..."

My hand mindlessly pressed the 'power off' button on the remote and the screen went black. I quickly surveyed the room around me, all eyes fixated on me clearly anticipating a reaction. I placed the remote control calmly on to the large wooden desk to my left before briskly walking toward the door. About four people yelled my name in response but I daren't turn around, I simply opened the door and left. I walked as fast as I could, passing office desks and windows of people who were now also gawking up at me. The news was travelling faster than I ever could have imagined and all I wanted to do was escape. I caught sight of the exit in the corridor ahead and pushed on forward when a sudden barrage of flashes and shouting startled me. There were masses of camera's and news crews set up outside yelling and screaming accusatory at me as my feet pounded the hard pavement. My heart was moments from truly exploding out of my chest from sheer surprise and terror of it all when I scrambled inside the tour bus and yelled at Calvin to drive. His eyes were wide with his own fear but he didn't question me, he simply buckled up and shoved the vehicle in to reverse, sounding the horn in a bid to shift the droves of people from the road. I hunkered down in one of the near bunks to try and compose myself. My breathing was rapid and my heart was palpitating. My phone had been buzzing non-stop inside my pocket since the moment I'd ran out the office. I placed my head in my hands and tried to gather my thoughts. What the fuck was happening. How quickly my life had flipped upside down. I didn't know where to begin or how to even start comprehending the situation I was in. The only person I kept thinking about was Lucy and her finding out about this. With my knees to my chest and crammed inside the bunk, I broke down.

A few hours later the bus pulled to a complete stop and I heard the engine die. I had no idea where we had driven to or how long I'd been sat hiding in the tiny bed compartment but it was darkening outside and the interior lights of the bus were in full glow. I stretched my limbs out from beneath me and swung my legs over the side of the bed, taking the slow walk back up to the front of the bus where I knew Calvin would be waiting. I plunked down in the passenger seat next to him but remained silent for a while longer. A few more precious moments passed before I worked up the courage to open my mouth.

"Where are we?" I asked groggily.

"Somewhere private," Calvin spoke softly, concern and compassion evident in his voice.

I nearly broke down again.

"Thank you," I barely whispered.

We remained seated, staring out at the view of the sea from the windscreen. The dark waves sloshed against the nearby rocks and the bridge up ahead stood mighty above it all. Seagulls swooped and dived at the frothy water, some catching fish and others coming up empty. I got lost in the simplicity of it all before my own reality began to sink in.

"Lucy's been calling," Calvin began and I felt the thickened lump in my throat.

"I reassured her that you're safe but she's obviously worried sick. You need to talk to her bro," He offered and I nodded, a silent tear escaped, betraying me.

I let out a shaky breath and closed my eyes before peeling my mobile from my pocket. My eyes glossed over the hundreds of text messages, missed calls and notifications that were angrily flashing up at me. I paid no mind to them, scrolling through my contacts until I found her name. I pressed the dial button and waited with baited breath. I had no idea how this was going to play out. She answered after one ring.

"Dylan, Dylan is that you?" Lucy cried in to the receiver.

"It's me," I responded trying in vain to hold it together.

"Dylan where are you? Please come home, please come home," her tears were choking her words.

"I'll be home soon, I promise," I sniffled, unable to hide my emotion.

"Be safe Dylan, I love you," Her voice rang in my ears.

"I love you too," I broke down then and hung up the phone.

Chapter 19

The weeping eventually subsided enough for me to hold a decent conversation. Calvin was my pillar. He asked the bare minimum and never expected anything in return. He listened to me. He believed me. So I wept some more. The realism and potential consequences of Iris's words were terrifying the life out of me. I'd seen enough news stories over the last year to know that once word got out about something like this your career was over. Dead in the water, whether the accusation was true or not. People did not care about the truth. People decided what they wanted to believe, irrelevant of the fact and right now, sexual assault allegations tarnished the reputation of men associated with them. A witch hunt would ensue and my family and friends would suffer as a consequence. My heart constricted again as I contemplated the devastating impact this would have on Lucy. On our future. On our unborn child. The reason I was deciding to call quits on the industry anyways. This was going to be our last big payday. One final album release, one final tour and all in the name of setting me and my family up for the rest of our lives. Iris had stolen that from me. From us. There was no way the record company were going to go ahead with the release or support us on a final show after this. The truth was meaningless and irrelevant. People were far too quick to jump to their own conclusions and sexual assault allegations carried a heavy price. It was almost as if Iris had carefully configured all of this to coincide with the end of my career. Our fifth and final album was due for release next month and the tour was three dates away from embarking on its final leg of the UK and European dates. Was she looking for revenge? It's the only plausible explanation I could muster for her hatred toward me. She never did handle our break up very well. But that was over fifteen years ago. I wasn't the same bastard as I was back then. And I had loved Iris. Just not the way I'd always loved Lucy.

Calvin graciously informed Trey and Rory of our current whereabouts, telling the other crew members and our agents that we were embarking on our long commute home via bus. The tour was now officially cancelled. The album release halted. And our lives practically on hold. The ride along with Calvin by bus would take a couple of days before we got back to England but I was grateful for the solitude and the chance to have my thoughts to myself for that moment longer. I knew there would be total carnage once we got back and I needed to be strong. Most importantly, I needed to be there for my wife. The only reason I had agreed to leave her in the first place had been for the sole purpose and prospect of returning with a nice chunky salary to see us through. With the tour now cancelled, I had no reason to be out here, stranded somewhere between France and Germany.

Calvin nipped to the nearest petrol station to top up and grab a few essential supplies for our journey. I slowly removed myself from the passenger seat and headed back towards the bunks. All of our gear was still here and I knew the boys would be waiting for me when we got back, eager for the belongings we hi-jacked and keen to hear my version of events. I shunned the thoughts, knowing that now was not the time. I needed to compose myself, recall my memories and get my affairs in order. I needed to focus on who and what was important. At thirty-six years of age I thought I'd had my fair share of heartache. I'd endured a shitty childhood and some devastating heartbreaks along the way. When the band achieved success and Lucy and I got married, I thought I'd escaped all of that. I could never have imagined another blow this low to befall me.

I stripped the current clothing from my back and shimmied out of my jeans, down to only my boxer shorts. I threw on a clean, plain grey t-shirt and a pair of khaki shorts. The ride was going to be a long one so I wanted to be as comfortable as possible. I grabbed my wireless headphones from the side desk and settled on a little respite to clear my head. The door of the bus swung open and Calvin reappeared with some bottles of water and snacks. He threw a couple of items my way and told me to get some rest. I nodded in appreciation. I placed the headphones over my ears and closed my eyes. The thronging sound of guitar strings enveloped my ears and the opening chords of "Love will tear us apart" by Joy Division washed over me. I leaned my head back on the pillow, no longer caring about the tears that continued to fall. I was owed this moment and I'd take it. Love was fucking brutal.

Chapter 20

October 1998

Today felt just like every other day. Only on this day, I was now legally of age to break away completely from this hell hole I'd spent the last eight years. My eighteenth birthday, to be precise had fallen on a Saturday and with little cash and even fewer friends I had only one thing on my mind. Escape. I lay staring at the ceiling of my shitty-ass bedroom and stared dreamily at the posters adorning the roof. My latest band's practise had been dreadful and I was strongly re-evaluating my passion for music. None of the guys put in any effort at all or even considered about taking the band or their instruments seriously. As such, we sounded like shit. It was disheartening. Why couldn't I be in a band with people who were equally as passionate about our sound as me? I sighed, running my hand over my face in a bid to relax my tension.

My phone buzzed then and a text lit up the screen. Lucy. I smiled.

"Happy birthday Dylan! 18!! How did you get so old?! Come over when you're ready, I have a surprise for you! xxx"

I snickered to myself. Of course she would. Typical Lucy. God only knows where I would be right now if it weren't for her. She helped me through some dark times these last few years. I'd repay the favour in a heartbeat. But Lucy was a good girl, and she knew better than to get herself involved with the sort of shit that I had done. Sure she was still a little young, fifteen to be exact but I doubted that she would ever stray in to bad shit like I had done. Okay, I wasn't exactly the devil, but I had done some pretty reckless things. I stretched out my limbs and slung my feet to the floor. A quick shower and change and I'd head over to her place. I only prayed I wouldn't bump in to any of the parental figures on the way.

I managed to escape the house without any issue and made my way over to where Lucy lived. Her parents were on holiday for the weekend and had left her alone with her big sister in charge. Lucy's sister Michelle was my age and we had shared a couple of classes together in high school. She never knew what her sister saw in me and openly made her feelings about me clear. She warned Lucy that I was bad news and that she should avoid me and my 'poisonous ways' but Lucy thankfully never listened. She was good like that. Always thinking for herself and never letting her decision be altered by anyone. Lucy and I were strictly friends and I'd never do anything to hurt her. Ever. She meant far too much to me. We'd been friends since she was eight years old. Back when my mother and father were together Lucy's dad and my dad had worked for the same company. We'd been invited over to a family BBQ at their house and that's how we came to meet. Ever since that day, Lucy and I had grown to have an unbreakable bond.

As I arrived at her house, the door automatically flung open and an enigmatic Lucy came bouncing out.

"Happy birthday!!" She screamed at me as she wrapped her arms around me.

"Thanks babe," I pecked her on the cheek, "But you didn't have to get me anything," I stated.

She shook her head and laughed like I'd told a joke. She grabbed my hand trailing me back inside the house.

"Where's Michelle?" I squinted around the place wondering what sort of insult I'd have to put up with when she saw me.

"She stayed out last night, new boyfriend I think," Lucy shrugged, seemingly unfazed at having her elder sister's whereabouts unconfirmed.

"So she left you here last night, on your own?" I winced, giving her my big brother stare.

Lucy smiled again.

"Calm down Dylan, I'm a big girl. I can take care of myself you know?" She hastened to add but I felt the unease in the pit of my stomach.

"If your sister doesn't come home today, be sure and text me. You're not spending the night alone again tonight you hear me?" I scolded her but she just laughed.

"You're funny Dylan, truly," she shook her head and her long hair fell around her face.

"Oh! Stay right there, be back in a minute!" She cried before dashing up the stairs.

I sighed wondering what the hell it was that she was so excited about. Truthfully, I could use some of her spunk. I hardly ever saw Lucy down. She was always cheerful and tried everything in her power to make me smile. I needed that these days. There had been too many years had passed with complete and utter sadness. Lucy was always a breath of fresh air.

"CLOSE YOUR EYES!" A voice yelled at me from the top of the stairs.

I snickered to myself before perching down on the living room sofa and closing my lids. The smile on my face palpable this time. What was she up to? A few thud noises later I sensed her presence.

"Okay," she breathed. "You can open them!"

I opened my eyes and caught a glimpse of her first, her eyes alight and her smile wide. Her hands were gesturing to a pile of goodies at the corner of the TV. One shape in particular caught my attention. I froze.

"Lucy?" I began but she shushed me immediately.

"Go on, open them!" She barked.

I slowly rose from my seat and headed towards the four wrapped gifts that were shining in my direction. I kneeled on the floor in front, unsure where to begin. 'The smallest first' I told myself.

I took the first box that was not much bigger than the palm of my hand and unwrapped it carefully. A clear packet inside with six letters inscribed. E A D G B E. A pack of guitar strings. I grinned. She knew me too well.

"Thanks a bunch babe, I really needed these!" I offered and Lucy just smiled.

I went on to open the next one. A rectangular box this time which felt really light. When I opened it up there was a rainbow coloured guitar strap with a few pins in place.

"Thought you could use a little colour you know when you're rehearsing?" Lucy teased and I stuck out my tongue at her.

Immature I know. It was a cute gift though. So her. It would always remind me of her for sure.

The third gift was incredibly heavy and square in shape. I unwrapped the gift to unveil a Marshall amplifier complete with leads and I stopped.

"Lucy, how the fuck did you get your hands on this?!" I exclaimed, my eyes not truly believing what they were seeing.

"I have my ways," She grinned so much I thought her cheeks would be hurting.

"This is *way* too much," I offered, my hands tracing over the box and trying to envision what kind of sound I could get from it.

"Don't be stupid D, it's your eighteenth birthday. It's a big deal!" She stated and her eyes glistened a little.

I swallowed hard. I was not prepared for this. I took a deep breath to try and make the feeling go away.

"Open the last one," she kneeled beside me this time before she spoke, gently nudging me in the shoulder.

The shape was clearly the outline of a guitar case that had also been expertly wrapped. I shuddered to think of what kind of expense Lucy had put herself through to retrieve these items for me. I knew she had a part time job but there was no way in hell she should have been splurging that hard earned cash on someone like me. It must have taken her months to save.

I swallowed again before my fingers got to work over the wrapping. The most beautifully hard-backed cherry-red guitar case with foam inserts was just beneath my fingertips. I shook my head unable to find the words.

"Lucy, I don't know what the fuck to say," I cursed.

"Don't say anything. Now you have everything you need to really get going. You're going to make it some-day Dylan, I promise. And you'll need these sorts of things for touring right?" She spoke innocently.

"Right," I repeated, my head still floating.

"Actually...There is one more thing," Lucy said and she stood.

"Impossible," I barked at her, unable to cope with the extravagance.
Lucy peered from around the door.

"You deserve this," she mouthed before she retrieved the object from the other side of the door.

A glistening, cherry red Ibanez guitar stared back at me.

My heart quickened.

"No," I spoke.

"Fuck no," I repeated.

"Yes!" She exclaimed.

"I can't accept that," I confirmed. I stood up from my kneeling position and backed away towards the window.

My hand resting uncomfortably on the back of my neck. I didn't know where to look.

"Dylan, Dylan!" Lucy cried. "Look at me, please," she pleaded.

She placed the instrument against the sofa and stepped toward me. Her short frame made her head eye level with my chest so she really had to look up at me to make eye contact. It would have been adorable had I not felt like the most conflicted guy on the planet. People like me were not entitled to lavish gifts from friends that were clearly too good for them.

"Dylan," she spoke again but this time she took my free hand in hers and placed her other hand on the side of my face so I could meet her eyes.

"You deserve this. After everything you've gone through in the past. You're destined to become so much more Dylan, I just know that. And deep down I want to give you the best fighting chance. This is my contribution. You can thank me when you're big and famous. You're going to make it babe, I can feel it in my bones!" She squealed and I couldn't help but laugh at her enthusiasm.

I didn't deserve her. Nobody did. Why couldn't I be more like her? She really broke the mould.

Knowing that I was fighting a losing battle I leaned down and enveloped my arms around her in the biggest bear hug imaginable. I breathed in her scent and swallowed hard. I'd never had someone believe in me as much as she had. Apart from Dana. But she'd been gone for over seven years now. I gripped her tightly, a fleet of emotions filtering through my head. I was overcome with gratitude at her generosity and her fight to believe in my worth. She may have only been fifteen years old but she was much wiser than her age dictated. I kissed her forehead.

Chapter 21

October 1997

I was only eleven years old when my sister Dana died. My mum and dad were continually arguing about who was at fault for months after the accident so I spent most of my days holed up in my room, praying for it all to end. I would sneak out of my room in the middle of the night and run the few streets it took to reach Lucy's. I climbed the drain pipe that ran from the ground to the roof a couple of inches from her bedroom window. One gentle tap on the glass and she would be there, greeting me with the biggest smile. I'd carefully scramble inside and we'd fall asleep in her bed, spooning each other like you would your favourite teddy bear. I'd always fall asleep to her tales of how we were both going to escape this place and become something more. She had a way of soothing me even when most days I felt like ripping the flesh from my bones just so I could feel something. I'd grown numb since the day my father broke the news that my sister would never be coming home.

My parents fighting only grew worse and only a year after Dana's passing, my father moved out. He fled the country and started a new family overseas. He checked in with me now and again over the phone but my teenage angst made it near impossible for us to have any sort of real bonding relationship. I grew bitter and resentful and dutifully tried to cut him out completely. My mother began drinking herself in to a stupor most nights and eventually got involved with a guy named Cody. Cody had a reputation for being a complete sleaze around the town and was known to frequently dabble in selling drugs. My mum failed to see the impact this would inevitably have and foolishly got remarried to the fucker. Cue beatings and abuse from stepdaddy.

As I grew older, the night time escapes to Lucy's grew less frequent. At fourteen years of age I hit puberty and being around girls, including Lucy, grew more difficult. My body was physically undergoing some serious changes and I also knew it could put our friendship in to some rocky territory so I didn't dare risk it. Lucy remained as innocent and bubbly as she always seemed to me up until she was around thirteen years of age. One afternoon after school, we decided to go to the local swimming pool to kill some time. When Lucy exited the changing room I couldn't help but stare at her new 'assets'. Two perfectly formed mounds were now adorning Lucy's chest. Her stomach and waist were somewhat lacking the little bit of puppy fat she'd carried through her early years and her hips were now suddenly more curvaceous. I wasn't sure how I hadn't noticed before but as she stood there in only her bikini there was no denying that she was on the cusp of womanhood. My little Lucy. It played havoc with my mind. My little innocent Lucy didn't look so innocent these days. Her school attire went from full uniform to a micro skirt, fitted blouse and knee high socks. Her hair, which she usually kept tied back was now down and lolling around her head in thick waves. Her lips had a clear shine and her eyes were highlighted with a pastel blue shadow and rimmed with eyeliner. She was growing up to be even more beautiful than I ever could have imagined. It unnerved me because I felt a compelling need to protect Lucy and shelter her from harm. She was a smart and beautiful girl but I knew all too well how quickly one bad decision could change all of that.

Through all of it though, our friendship always remained. Some months we naturally grew more distant than others. Lucy always made a point to text me or come speak to me at school if too many weeks had passed by so that we could catch up. Our conversations were always animated and joyous despite the hushed whispers and disgusting comments from some of our peers and onlookers. It seemed kids at our school couldn't deal with the fact that a guy and girl could simply be friends. Maybe it was the contrast between Lucy's popularity and how much of a waster I appeared that they couldn't handle. Or maybe it was the age difference. Either way Lucy was unfazed, which only continued to prove to me that she was above all of this. No one deserved her. Least of all me.

At sixteen years old and three years her senior after all, I had already began experimenting with drink and recreational drugs. I spent evenings after school hanging behind local stores and smoking weed with some of the nervy kids from school. A few of those guys had mentioned something about wanting to start a band so naturally I was inclined to join. We jammed in one of their parent's basements as often as we could and smoked and drank just to pass the time by. I knew Lucy had concerns about my new friendships and behaviour changes but she never commented or judged me. I loved her for that. More deeply than she'd ever know. She was my constant. While she was growing up and having girly sleepovers which I imagined were rich with boy talk and romantic movie marathons, I was homing in on my guitar skills, getting high and eventually experimenting with girls. Anyone willing to come down to the basement to 'hear us play' or drink with us inevitably ended up in the sack. I knew the rumours around school were rife but it didn't deter the number of teenage girls willing to be a part of that scene or willing to spread their legs for that matter. I took my fill. Literally. It killed the time. It busied my mind. It was a distraction.

I'd reached the end of my fourth year at school and was a few months from my seventeenth birthday when my mum dropped the bombshell I'd been dreading. In one of our very few conversations she yelled at me;

"You need to leave school and get a real job! You have to start paying bills around here. Cody said you're a man now and it's time to start pulling your weight! Rent is due by Friday. If you're gonna keep living here I want fifty quid a week!" blah blah blah.

A *real* job?! That was rich coming from an alcoholic housewife who sat on her arse all day watching T.V. and a drug dealing stepfather who was out at all hours doing god only knows what. The beatings had thankfully subsided since I was now taller than Cody and stronger than him, well at least most days. He occasionally would catch me off guard by throwing a heavy object at me while I slept on my bed or punching me in the face when I had my headphones on and my back was turned. He was such a fucking coward. His outbursts usually led to him bloodying my nose or giving me a black eye in his rage which left me explaining to the teaching faculty about how 'clumsy' I am. I didn't doubt for a minute that they saw right through me. Most were just too afraid to deal with the truth. They knew if they took it up further they risked a personal retaliation from Cody and his posse. And a teaching salary was hardly worth the hassle.

So at the request of my mother and the apparent demand from my stepfather I had to drop out of school. No college opportunity, no summer trip to music school, despite an acceptance letter offering me a funded position and no means to escape their clutches. Yet. I vowed that I would graft until I'd saved enough money to move out on my own. I wanted to pursue a music career and I would never allow them to hold me back.

As I refilled another coffee cup and wiped down the spilled milk from the counter I caught my reflection in the metallic urn. My ridiculous green uniformed cap shielding most of my face and my hair peeking out just above my ears. I knew it needed a trim but I refused to pay for a haircut right now. I was penny pinching as if my life depended on it because in some ways it did. Besides, Lucy had offered to cut it for me at our next meet up. Which was exactly a week from today. My seventeenth birthday. I stared hard at the urn once more, unable to recognise the scowl. How the fuck had I ended up here? A coughing sound from behind me reminded me that I was in the middle of serving and my customer had obviously grown impatient. Fuck him and fuck this place. I wiped the over-filled coffee mug and then brought the steaming cup to the man at the till. Quickly throwing on my best apologetic smile in a bid to get whatever tips I could. Fake it 'til you make it right? Or so they say.

Chapter 22

September 2016

Once the bus arrived in England, I called a local taxi company and made arrangements with them to get me back home. I bid Calvin a temporary farewell as I exited the bus and he wished me luck before he drove off, presumably to deliver the rest of the guy's belongings.

The taxi driver hadn't seemed to recognise me and for that I was eternally grateful. I wasn't prepared to deal with talking to anyone other than Lucy right now and I really needed to be with her. As we neared my address, a swarm of vehicles were parked along both sides of the streets. Camera crews and news reporters were stationed just outside my garden gate. My pulse quickened, my throat constricted and my knuckles had whitened. The taxi driver scanned the area and whistled before passing comment;

"Well, well I wonder what's going on in that gaff?" He cocked his head and then quickly his expression changed as he registered the address.

His face fell and he looked at me warily.

"How much do I owe you," I spoke through gritted teeth.

I needed this transaction to be over and quick. Us drawing up had already caused a stir with some of the waiting press.

"Uhhh, that'll be eleven pounds eighty," the man stumbled over his words a little trying to comprehend what he had just let himself in to.

I threw a twenty at him and put on my sunglasses.

"Keep the change," I cried before exiting the vehicle.

I held my coat tightly around my chin and kept my head lowered as I waded through the crowd.

"Dylan, Dylan!" they yelled my name over and over.

"Dylan, what's your response to the current sexual allegations being brought to you from Iris?" One yelled as I walked as fast as possible to the garden gate.

"How does your wife feel knowing you molested a girl who was underage?" I cringed, my stomach feeling like I could throw up at any moment.

"What will become of The Attachment Theory since you've departed ways?" I took a deep breath.

Once I'd made it past the gate and up the path I breathed a sigh of relief at the sight of my front door. I shunned the last of the throw away questions, comments and abuse being hurled at me and turned the handle. Once inside, I quickly slammed it behind me and then locked the door.

I dropped my backpack to the floor and took off my sunglasses, unfastening my coat and dropping it to the ground with the rest of my items. I raised my head and caught sight of Lucy. My beautiful Lucy standing at the foot of the stairwell, her dark hair just as I remembered, the growing swell of her stomach bigger since I'd last seen her and her eyes focused on me. She was a little distance away but I could still see the utter pain and devastation in them and the obvious bags where she'd been crying and not sleeping. The pain in them only made my own heart ache more. I swallowed hard. Of all the things I had and could have endured in this lifetime, breaking her heart was the one I had vowed never to do. Yet here we were.

I moved cautiously toward her, unsure of what to expect in response. As I neared, her arms reached out for me and I welcomed them as if it was the air I needed to breathe. I grabbed hold of her, gripping her tightly but being mindful of putting any extra pressure on the bump between us. She relaxed in to me, a sob escaping her just then and I knew this was going to be the hardest few days of my life. I bit back my own urge to cry, I'd shed enough tears the last few days and I promised myself I would be the strong one. We were going to get through this. I needed to make sure Lucy refrained from worry so that her and the baby could be safe. I breathed in her scent and stroked her hair affectionately, shushing her reassuringly.

She peered up at me through thick, dark, soaked lashes. Her eyes scanned my face as if she were trying to read something in them.

"Are you okay?" she asked softly and I nodded.

"I am now," I breathed, stroking the side of her cheek and caressing her tummy.

"Everything's falling apart! How did we get here, Dylan?" She asked, trying to piece together the string of current events with the ones from the past.

I took a deep breath.

I thought about the what I could say to try and make sense of it all but nothing seemed apt. It was clear from the little I'd heard on the news that Iris had gone public about her relationship with me all those years ago. That I couldn't disagree with. We had been together. We'd shared some intimate moments together. She'd given her virginity to me. I also left her for Lucy. When I say left I actually meant cheated on. I wasn't proud of that fact but it was the truth. The truth I knew, Iris knew and Lucy knew. Even Reece, Lucy's ex-boyfriend if I recalled correctly. If Iris felt the need to reveal these details after so many years, then so be it. But that's not what plagued me. What troubled me was the accusation of her being underage during those years. She had been seventeen. I remembered her specifically telling me her age when we'd first conversed and also reading an article printed about her on the college web page that stated so. She was over the legal age of consent in this country. Her theory that I had groomed her or mislead her in anyway was total fucking bullshit. Iris had been a willing participant at every step of the way. I made sure of it. I always maintained I was no angel but I was no fucking paedophile either. Yet, Iris had managed to twist her version of our story in to one that painted me as such. That cruel bitch.

Lucy was studying my face once more, obviously concerned by my silence.

"Honestly babe, I have no clue. I don't even know what's triggered all of these lies," I replied bleakly.

"But I assure you, that's what they are. Lies." I hastened to add.

Lucy nodded.

"Do you think she's trying to seek some kind of revenge against us or something? For catching us like she did?" Lucy whispered, her hands gripping around me lovingly.

"Fuck knows sweetie. It seems a little extreme don't you think? We were all so young back then. But please don't you worry about it. I'll get this shit sorted. ASAP," I added as convincingly as I could.

I kissed her forehead and she gave a sweet smile.

How I'd missed her face.

Although a part of me felt devastated at the sudden and abrupt finality of my career in The Attachment Theory, my priorities were clear and they were right here in my arms. I would give up everything to ensure their happiness and safety and if that's what it would take to get through this then so be it. I'd sacrifice it all for them. Lucy and my child were all the family I'd ever need. A new urge of determination coursed through me.

Chapter 23

After another uneasy night's rest, Lucy had kindly set up an appointment with our family solicitor to help us deal with the ongoing accusation. We hadn't formally been summoned to any court hearings as of yet but we were being extra cautious and discussing all of our options in preparation in case it came to that. My gut instinct warned me that Iris had a plan to take this as far as she could. She wouldn't be satisfied with purely dragging my name through the mud. If that was the case, she would have been happy labelling me a cheater. Instead, she wanted a massive public affair. I knew how manipulative and vindictive she could be when she wanted to get her own way. There was little
that would stop her once her mind was set.

My mind brought forth a past memory.

It was sometime around April in 2004 and I'd just come home from a long and tiring gig. Me and the boys had been drinking throughout the night and I was exhausted. I was ready for bed. I glanced at my phone screen while unlocking the door. It was already past one am. No wonder I was shattered. I turned the handle and practically jumped out of my skin at the screech ringing in my ears.

"Surprise!" Iris yelled as soon as I'd entered my apartment door.

"Fucking hell Iris," I clutched my chest, trying to calm my nerves.

Although we'd been seeing one another for over two years we'd only made it official over the last few months. I still, however, wasn't comfortable with how often she allowed herself access to my place. I should have guessed Iris had made other plans. So much for my early night then.

"Is that any way to speak to your girlfriend?!" She yelled at me, her eyes furrowed and her arms crossed over her chest.

She was dressed in one of my tee's and a pair of my boxer shorts, clearly having made herself at home. Part of me didn't mind. The other part, it was irate.

"Shit, sorry Iris. I'm just knackered that's all," I closed the door behind me.

I was in no humour for whatever game I knew she would insist on playing. Not tonight. My head was way too fucked up to even muster the energy to feign interest. I only prayed she would take the hint.

She stood with her bottom lip jutting out, pouting. I gave her a brief hug and kissed the side of her cheek.

Her arms remained folded against her body.

"Is that it?" She spat.

Here we go.

"I put in all the effort to come over here to your dull ass apartment, wait for hours until you've finished some shitty gig and then you greet me with a mere kiss on the fucking cheek?" Her voice was venomous.

"Iris don't, we've been through this. I never asked for you to come over or for you to hang around waiting for my return. You knew I'd be late in getting home and I'm shattered! My intention was to catch up on sleep. Please don't make this some sort of deal about you," I knew the last statement would come back to bite me in the ass.

I turned from her and slumped down on the couch, my fingers pinching the bridge of my nose. I wasn't prepared for this.

"Of course it's not about me, because it's always about you! Isn't that right Dylan? So come on then, who the fuck is she?" She marched in front of where I sat, gazing down at me with fire in her eyes.

I shook my head incredulously at yet another accusation. I wished I could say I'd grown used to it by now but the fact was it still hurt that she thought so little of me. I'd actually treated Iris with nothing but love and respect since the moment we made it official. Yes, there were constant offers and invites from the fairer sex on several occasions but I always politely declined. It was part of the territory that came with being a band member. The more well-known our music became, the more our fan-base grew. As did the wannabe groupie ring. That was simply the natural order of things.

I never pinned Iris as being the jealous type when we'd first met but oh how wrong I was. Within a few months she made it abundantly clear to any and all females who as much looked at me after a show to steer clear. She even snapped at me for my relationship with Lucy but I didn't let that one slide. She could bitch and moan about any random as she saw fit but she would never come between me and my best friend and I told her as much. She wasn't happy about it but she sensed the touchiness of it all and decided to leave it alone. At least for now. I didn't have the heart to share that information with Lucy. She was far too lovable and important in my life to bombard her with petty matters from a jealous soul. Even if the jealous soul was my so called 'girlfriend'. Fuck. I don't know how the hell I got here. I never wanted to be in a relationship, let alone play babysitter to someone whose mood swings were so extreme you'd think she suffered from bi-polar disorder. Maybe she did. Maybe there was rationale behind her outrageous actions and accusatory benders.

Either way, I hated feeling like a piece of property but that was the control she had over me. I was blindsided by her innocence and beauty in the beginning but those feelings were slowly converting into strenuous battles of trying to prove trustworthy and downplaying any interactions I had with people that weren't her. It was unnatural. I'd considered myself social and pretty laidback until recently. Yes, I'd suffered from severe depression in my early teens but the band and my life away from my parents had put me in a much better mental state. I very rarely had anxiety issues like I once did and I most certainly hadn't conjured any real negative and dark thoughts like I used to. I was in a good place. I just needed to maintain it. That's what scared me the most about Iris. I wasn't wholly convinced that she was exactly good for me and my well-being.

I now dreaded the aftermath of a show where a fan got their tits out or a girl gave me a sweet note about how much we meant to them. Iris would flip out and lash out and even hit me. It clouded every positive vibe that came with all the hard-work we'd put in to recording and our live performances. I remember when she used to love coming to the shows and I loved seeing her there, snapping away with her camera and smiling up at me adoringly. Now she barely ever took her camera from its resting place under my bed and she never once commented on how our shows had gone down. I was completely conflicted internally. I'd grown exhausted.

But even through all of the seemingly tireless negativity that we'd gone through, Iris had a way of reeling me back in. There was something so seductive in the way she worked her body for me. Pure adrenaline would race through me at her every move. She knew just what I liked and how to get me off quicker than most had ever even come close and for that, I was hooked. It was catharsis for my soul. On days where shit felt too heavy, a night spent fucking with Iris would clear my head. We'd tried all sorts and she was always keen to keep experimenting. Hard to believe that she'd been a virgin before her encounter with me a few years back. I think that's also why I admired her. I was her first and only fuck. Ever. And she'd remained with me throughout. There was something humbling in the idea of being enough for someone. Good enough. I still felt worthless on a good day though. My step-dad made sure to leave that embedded in my head. A counsellor would have a field day with me, I swear.

I peered up at the seething woman before me and tried to weigh up my options. My early night was clearly no longer viable and I thought it best to try and diffuse her anger before it got too deep. Better yet, I could turn her anger in to something else. You know what they say about a woman scorned and all that.

"Iris, please. There is no one else. You know I would never do that to you. I promise," I rose to my feet.

I approached her carefully and softly put my lips against hers.

Iris may have known just how to get me off but I had a few tricks of my own too. She was still susceptible in succumbing to my charms.

I kissed her once and gazed deep in to her eyes.

"Iris," I breathed out her name.

She kept her eyes averted.

"Iris, look at me," I demanded her attention, voice gruff and a spark instantly flared as she caught my eye, realisation beckoning.

"Are you disobeying me?" I held her cheeks between my palms and she smiled.

"Go to the bedroom and strip. I want to see you on that bed, with your hands above your head and your legs spread, wide. Do it. Now!" I scolded.

She grinned, that devious looking smile etched across her face before she practically skipped in the direction of the bedroom.

We had always endeavoured to keep our sex life as varied as possible and adhered to a variety of roleplay over our time together. But Iris had a favourite, even if she never truly admitted it to herself. Submissive. She was always a sucker for playing the submissive. She couldn't fight off a dominant Dylan even if she wanted to.

I ran a weary hand through my hair and tossed my t-shirt to the side.

Exhausted but trying to salvage what I could of my strength, I set off after her. Like a master drawn to his slave.

Chapter 24

Our solicitor spoke frankly, gathering our version of events from the time period in question and making note of any other people we knew who could vouch for our whereabouts and alibi's if they were ever brought in to question. He assured us that until I was formally charged of course, everything else was purely hearsay and speculation. He did make a point to remind me that if I were to be found guilty of any wrongdoing from my past, a historic sex charge involving sleeping with a minor could carry up to two years' worth of jail time, including having my name remain on the sex offenders list. I shuddered at the thought but quickly dismissed it knowing fine well that Iris would have some serious difficulty in trying to verify her story. Right now it was her word against mine. But in court, I was more than willing to bring forth what was required to clear my name and prove my innocence. If it came to that.

The reporters from yesterday had reduced slightly in number. I convinced Lucy it was best for us all if we remained indoors and avoided them at all cost. Until we knew exactly where we stood in all of this, there was no current need to issue a statement. Besides, people made a living doing just that. Our PR people could handle all items relating to the band on my behalf until my name was cleared. I'd spoken with both Trey and Rory over the phone today who had assured me that they were on my side and would defend me and give proof if required. I thanked them both profusely for their support and apologised for how I'd left things a few days ago. They reassured me that they understood my reasoning and were happy to hold back until everything had died down. The future of the band was in jeopardy but that wasn't my focus right now.

After a quiet dinner and some small talk about potential baby names, a knock on the door broke Lucy and I from our reverie. Her eyes worriedly caught mine, a panic in them that spoke volumes. I urged her to remain calm and begged her to allow me to handle it.

I strode over to the front door anxiously, and inhaled sharply before turning the handle to open the door. A parcel delivery driver held a box in one hand and an electronic signing device in the other.

"Delivery for Mr Wakefield," he held the questionable box toward me and I reluctantly accepted it.

I scribbled a signature on his device and thanked him before he departed. I hurriedly locked the door again to avoid any unwanted attention and headed back towards the dining table. Lucy looked up at me expectantly.

"What's that?" She motioned to the cardboard box nestled against my chest.

"I'm not sure," I replied warily.

My gut told me to refrain from opening but curiosity got the better of me. I needed to know what was inside.

I grabbed a knife from a nearby drawer and pierced the brown parcel tape carefully. Unfolding the flaps cautiously at first, I peered inside. Lucy's eyes were still fixed on me.

I unearthed the contents of the box with two hands and laid down a giant stack of paper notes on the table. I furrowed my brow trying to figure out what sat before me. The handwritten note on the front of the mound was instantly recognisable.

"Tales from a tortured submissive" by Iris Steadman.

Bile rose in my throat.

My eyes quickly scanned over the additional paper insert and found a typed letter that was addressed specifically to me. I quickly snatched it away and hid it in my back pocket before Lucy had a chance to see it.

She rose from her seat, coming to study what had left me speechless.

I flicked through what seemed to be a lengthy manuscript detailing intimate and perverse details in a 'tell-all' style auto-biography which no doubt named and shamed me as some sort of manipulative abuser.

"Dylan?" Lucy frowned, resting a slight hand on her lower back as support for her ever growing bump.

"It's nothing, please, let's just let the solicitor deal with it," I hastened to add, hurriedly trying to shove the horrid white printed words in to the hellish box they sprung from.

Lucy quickly snatched the top sheet and read the title aloud.

"'Submissive?" She glared at me, "Is that what she was to you?" Her voice grew shaky.

"Lucy please, let's just forget about it. She's trying to fuck with our heads," I urged but it was no use.

I could see the cogs in motion as she began pondering about the kind of relationship I had shared with my accuser. Lucy and I had discussed most of our personal moments in very thorough detail but when it came to Iris, I consciously withheld some of the more extreme practises of our sexual escapades to save both me and her from embarrassment. Now, I feared that my failure to disclose those facts would leave Lucy questioning my role and my actions in the past. My head pounded with the stress from it all.

"You can't just suddenly produce an entire books worth of material from thin air Dylan. There's obviously more to this than you're letting on," she began and I could already hear the change of tone in her voice.

Lucy was always so complacent and calm even in my most earth-shattering moments she'd been the one to steer me from my rage. Hearing her about to lose her cool was making my skin crawl.

"Please, Lucy you've got it all wrong. Iris thrives on attention; she always has done. She wants this to be as dramatic as possible and is therefore taking joy in seeing us suffer. Don't give in to her wants. She'll be hoping that we fight over this," I begged Lucy to see some rationale before she erupted but it was like pushing against the tide when the banks had already burst.

"Give me the box Dylan," she barked and I could see the rage hidden behind her glistening eyes.

I shook my head firmly, hands clasped either side of the cardboard knowing that the moment I let it go, the rest of my life may as well slip away with it.

"I have a right to know what she's saying about my husband. Hand it over. Now," and her tiny frame suddenly seemed menacing in the dimly lit dining room.

I let out a defeated sigh and slid the box toward her, my heart beating so hard I thought my chest might implode.

"Please don't over think this Lucy and for god sake don't take it all literal," I spoke softly as I placed a hand on top of hers protectively. "Iris was and clearly still is a fantasist. I bet half of what she's written in here is completely fictional anyways," I finished but Lucy remained silent.

Instead she responded by picking up the box stubbornly and strolling off toward the sitting room where I knew she would spend the entire evening mulling over whatever words Iris had penned in those sheets of paper.

Words that had the power to change someone's perception of me in a heartbeat. I prayed that Lucy was not so easily swayed.

Chapter 25

I sat hunched over my old wooden desk with a pen in hand, letting the ink spill hurriedly across the crisp, white page. My lyrics had always reflected a deeper and more personal side of me that I never really felt comfortable sharing verbally before. It always amazed me what thoughts would make themselves known if you simply allowed them a quiet moment to appear.

For years now, these darkened room ramblings had helped shape and build the core of our musical back catalogue. Writing lyrics and making music was my way of dealing with an internal demon that I felt I could no longer harbour. Although the likelihood of me ever allowing these words to see the light of day was slim, I continued to be a slave to the format of penning those words because it was habitually how I had dealt with troubles over the last fifteen years.

I recalled the feeling of being conflicted when our fans would reach out and remind me of how much they said they related with my words. Pride for the most part that I had managed to establish a connection with them over the soundwaves and then a complete wash of sadness as I contemplated their meaning. My lyrics were never an easy ride. They detailed inner feelings I kept mostly hidden about depression and suicidal thoughts. A longing of wanting to feel free when I evidently was not.

On the outside I appeared charming and I would croon my way in to the hearts of thousands of listeners. All the while, my insides were plagued with anxiety, self-doubt and self-loathing. They had been since I was a child. I wouldn't have wished my most negative feelings on my worst enemy, let alone an avid fan. My heart ached for those who felt they could even remotely relate.

A knock on the door caught me off guard. The slow creaking noise from the hinges filled the dimly lit room.

"Hi," Lucy almost whispered, her slender arms prising the door closed behind her.

"Hey," I replied nervously, placing my pen down and quickly closing the leather-clad notebook in front of me.

"Sorry for disturbing you," She apologised, her chocolate brown eyes glazing over with a compassion that as an artist I could spend three albums mulling over.

"It's fine, I was just finishing up," I lied, desperate to take the heat off for a moment.

"I uh," She cleared her throat, "I finished Iris's book, if that's what you want to call it," she stated coolly and my pulse quickened.

I had no idea how this was going to play out.

"And?" I prompted, desperate to know where her mind was currently given the situation.

"I think you should read it," she spoke and I furrowed my brow in confusion.

"What?" I asked incredulously.

Iris's words were not what I wanted to get plagued down with. I had much more pressing matters at hand. I shuddered at the thought.

"Please, for me," She amended.

I felt confusion wash over me.

I couldn't fathom what good could possibly come of her request. But seeing as I had very little choice, I caved.

"If it's what you want, then I'll read it. For you," I confirmed and she smiled.

"Thanks. Let me know when you're done. I'm going for a bath. See you in a bit," she spoke, her voice sounding tired.

She leaned toward me and placed a gentle kiss on my cheek before exiting my study.

It terrified me. It's as if she were saying goodbye.

I sighed, my hands gripping my forehead torturously with pent up emotion. That's when I remembered about the note.

I reached in to the back pocket of my jeans and produced the typed letter I'd managed to snag from the box earlier. Taking a deep breath, I unfolded it and glanced at the words.

"I forgive you for what you've taken from me but I will never forget.
And nor will the world.
See you in court.

Love Iris x"

I scrunched up the piece of paper furiously and clasped my hands in to two fists. I closed my eyes and tried to breathe through my impending rage.

I always said Iris Steadman would be the death of me.

Chapter 26

December 2017

I watched the waves momentarily as they lapped at the shore and felt the chill from the cooling breeze. I wrapped my arms securely around my chest trying to muster whatever little warmth I could. My black fitted t-shirt did little to keep any heat in against the harsh winter air so I shivered even more when my cool hands brushed against the inside of my biceps. I tried hugging myself some more but there was absolutely no comfort in it.

The crushed pebbles gave way beneath my feet as I stepped even closer to the raging sea. The water now soaking through my converse shoes and pooling around the ankles of my jeans. I could see no other way.

With my arms still around me, I edged even deeper and deeper into the icy cold liquid. I tried my best to compose my balance as the wind whipped around me, growing much fiercer the further I waded in.

With the water quickly around waist height my teeth began to chatter. My hands were now slung either side of my body, my fingers splayed out so that they delicately skimmed the tip of the water beneath me.

My breathing intensified as more and more water surrounded me. The splash back from oncoming waves drenching me. I could feel the dark locks of my hair matting against my forehead.

"Not much further now," I told myself.

My mind focused on the roar of the sea and the echoing sound of water sloshing around me. I willed my trembling body to venture even further still, the water line circling my shoulders. My tears mixing with the salty water, making them indistinguishable from the sea that was inches from consuming me for good.

In the distance, I think I can hear my name being called but I'm too far gone to contemplate turning around now.

I need this to be over.

I can no longer bury myself in pain.

My breathing comes in short, rapid successions, the water beneath my chin as I close my eyes.

One deep and final breath away from total immersion and I will finally be cleansed of all of my fears and worries.

No more anxiety, no more fear.

No more pain or inflicting it on those I loved.

No more feeling like a burden.

No more heartache.

To be at peace, once and for all.

I smile to myself contently, before the oncoming wave engulfs me.

Epilogue

February 2018

I stared at the mass of unfamiliar faces in the circle, making sure I listened carefully to what the speaker had to say. I'd never been to a support group before so I had no idea what to expect. My first impressions were instinctually dismissed after hearing several of the other members share stories about their lives.

So much pain and suffering shared between these four walls. I involuntarily shivered as my mind tried to remain focused on the task at hand.

Tonight was not just about them. It was about me. It was about trying to accept what had happened and move on from the past. I glanced around at the curious faces once more before hearing my name being called out.

"Iris," The speaker smiled. "Why don't you share your story with the rest of the group tonight. Please know that you have our undivided attention and support through-out this process," she beamed and I grew even more nervous.

I smiled back at her, falsely of course since I no longer knew how to really feel other than numb, before taking a deep breath.

"Hey everyone," I began, "My name is Iris Steadman,"

"Hello Iris," everyone chanted, a barrage of monotone voices.

"I'm here because I'm having trouble moving past a tragedy that occurred last year involving someone who I loved dearly," I breathed, palming my hands against the fabric covering my thighs.

"You see, for the last fifteen years or so, I've been harbouring some pretty negative thoughts. I'm not proud of that fact, but I want to make others aware of just how impactful those negative thoughts can be, not only to ourselves, but to others."

All of the other's eyes were on me, listening, intrigued. I willed myself to let the words flow.

"Many years ago, I had my heart broken by a man who I felt I couldn't live without. I caught him cheating on me with his best friend at the time and never really learned how to deal with my feelings.

Instead of facing up to what had happened, I hid away. I hid away long enough to conjure up a horrid plot for my revenge.

You see, I wanted to make him suffer just like I had. I needed him to feel the hurt he had inflicted upon me. I was angry and devastated and stupidly young. He was my first and only true love. I could see no other way.

So, for the better part of a decade I concocted a devious plan that would tear this man's world apart.

I sat in the shadows while the man I loved moved on with his life as though I never really existed. I watched him achieve fame and success and marry his best friend. I sat through countless conversations with work colleagues and friends who admired him and spoke about him as if he were god-like all the while knowing he had destroyed my chance at a happy future.

I got so bitter that I became depressed and suffered countless breakdowns.

Fifteen years of battling the will to live and plotting the ultimate mark for revenge.

Needless to say my timing couldn't have been more perfect," I paused.

My hands grew clammy so I rubbed them against my jeans once more.

"The man in question was on the brink of a career high and was about to give up his fame in exchange for a quiet and settled life with his wife and his unborn child.

I couldn't keep silent any longer.

So I starting speaking to people around me and posting online about my former relationship with this man, telling anyone who would listen about how I knew him before his success and that we'd been intimate. Everyone was revelling in the idea of getting first hand gossip about someone they had grown to idolise and then suddenly, I had found my platform. The more people who listened the more my story grew. Once I knew I had some serious attention I took it as my opportunity to do what I'd always planned.

I spread the rumour that I had been underage during our sexual relationship.

One tiny little lie that spread like wildfire." I grimaced.

Some of the group member's eyes diverted away from me subconsciously, clearly uneasy in my re-hashing of events. I didn't let it dispel me from continuing with my story. It was just the beginning after all;

"Once word got out about my age, the man in question's reputation plunged drastically. He lost a record deal, sponsorship, touring privileges and eventually the entire band he'd achieved fame with had to call it quits. There was so much backlash and hate from fans that they could no longer justify the continuation of what they were doing.

I thought it would have been enough for his wife to leave him.

But I was wrong.

Even though everything else around him was falling apart, she stood by him every step of the way. My plan to corrupt her view of him and terminate their relationship had failed.

Unsatisfied with this, I decided to pursue things further."

I coughed a little, in a bid to clear my throat. The group remained silent.

"I then spent two months holed up in my apartment drafting a supposedly auto-biographical account of the relationship I'd had with this man before he had become successful. I shared my most intimate sexual experiences, some of which were true and others that were not. I included a detailed passage on how I lost my virginity to him at the age of fifteen. It was in part, truthful. He had been my first sexual partner. The other half however, was of course a lie. I had in fact been seventeen at the time. Not fifteen as I'd lead the press to believe. Two years. Two years that made all the difference.

In my account of events I had painted an obscure picture of the man I loved as being dominant, abusive and controlling. I retold of our sexual encounters but added my own fictional spin on them to make him seem animalistic and addictive. I created a monster for the world to despise and share in my hatred for him. To top it all off I gained the public's sympathy by detailing a fictional account of a forced abortion I had supposedly undertaken at age sixteen. Yet another terrible lie," and I heard one of the women at the far right of the group gasp.

I closed my eyes momentarily, ashamed at my actions.

"It hadn't mattered that it was a lie at the time of course. Word against word. Mines against his. And in this current world we live in, people are always keen to assume their own truths. No one thought to doubt or discredit me. No one even questioned the legitimacy of my version of events so much so that legally I was inundated with offers of representation in a court of law and urged to take my case against him seriously.

In a last bid attempt to destroy the life of the man I'd loved, I shipped my final draft of the proposed book to his house, the night before it was to be published and released to the public. I prayed that once his wife had read first hand my account of supposed events that took place all those years ago, that she would see the light and leave him. Making him suffer just as much as I had done. Being pregnant made her vulnerable and I prayed on that by adding the fake abortion story in my manuscript. I never really imagined the impact or the power my words would have on another human being before.

And begrudgingly so, my plan worked.

From what I read in the newspapers, shortly after the release of my novel his wife left their marital home. It seemed she was unable to live with the possibility that her husband may have kept a dark secret in his past and the marriage suffered as a consequence. As such, she quickly filed for divorce and was granted full custody rights of their daughter."

I swallowed. I took another deep breath.

"I remember when I first read the article I expected to feel joy. Instead, the first thing I felt was grief. Thinking about ripping this man's family apart and actually successfully achieving it were two very different things. I felt sick at knowing my actions had impacted in such a way and felt shame at how out of control I had let it all get.

I tried to contact news and press and retract some of my statements, feeling ready to fess up about my version of events but by then it was too late. People had already made up their mind and my former lover was now almost penniless and alone. He became a recluse after suffering a barrage of abuse online, at his home and even in the streets from the public backlash. His wife leaving him somehow made other's deem my words to be true. He was alone and fearful and left with nothing but his own mind.

And just when I thought things couldn't get any worse, they did."

I could no longer hold back the tears that were streaming down my cheeks at this point.

I took a deep breath and braced myself.

I needed to say the words out loud.

"On Sunday morning, 12th of December 2017, the love of my life committed suicide." I inhaled sharply.

I felt the faces around me stiffen and gasp.

"His name was Dylan Wakefield. He was thirty- eight years old,".

The room grew deathly still. There was no other sound except for my sniffling as the tears continued to cascade down my face.

I lowered my head in complete and utter shame.

Awash with devastation.

Silence fell over the room once more and the man next to me pressed his hand in to my own, squeezing it reassuringly, urging me to continue.

I didn't deserve the kindness in his gesture.

"My words ultimately drove an innocent man in to taking his own life. That was the power bestowed in me all because of a shitty lie. All because of a stupid, jealous and angry little girl who couldn't deal with her heartache in the traditional sense," I wept.

"I never asked for help. Instead, I let my hatred fester to an unstoppable force that ultimately led to Dylan's death. I tore a man apart, piece by piece and watched it all play out live in front of thousands. I could have spoken up at any time. I could have retracted statements. I could have reached out to his estranged wife and owned up to the truth, salvaging their relationship.

There are so many things that I could have done, but instead I remained silent. Silent when the truth really mattered.

I don't think I will ever be able to forgive myself for what I've done. I have even contemplated taking my own life countless times," I sniffle.

"But it still does not give the man the justice he deserves. I sit here, among you today to try and do that. I'm here to urge everyone to think long and hard about the impact that your words and actions or lack thereof, have on the people around you.

You can never know for certain what's going on in another individual's mind. But people are fragile, and we all have our breaking point.

Let's try to mend each other instead of break each other," I wipe at my eyes with the back of my hoodie sleeve.

The room begins applauding but it feels inadequate and inappropriate.

I have no idea how this was supposed to help me deal with my current mental state but my doctors have urged me to reach out to people and try talking about my past as if it will somehow make the guilt go away.

The speaker thanked me for sharing and the group quickly moved on to the next tortured soul.

I listen politely and remain seated until the end of the session.

A few months later I find myself walking swiftly out of the same annexed building that I'd now spent every week attending regular meetings in before settling in the direction of home.

The chilly spring air creeps across my skin and reminds me that winter isn't finished with me yet but my walk is brisk and my apartment comes in to view a few moments later.

A womanly presence outside my door has my heart racing as I approach.

Recognition of the woman in question has my blood pulsating in my ears so badly that I turn on my heel and attempt to flee, but her voice stops me dead in my tracks.

"Iris, wait! I don't want any trouble!" she beckons.

I'm paused with my back to her and I'm too terrified to even contemplate turning around.

It's like I'm frozen in place.

Lucy's hand graces my shoulder as she spins me around. My own hands instantaneously reach up to shield my face, anticipating the impact that was sure to come.

Lucy holds both her palms up in surrender, making it clear that she hasn't come here to fight. At least not in the street.

I compose myself before studying her features.

She's surprisingly calm as she wraps her woollen coat around her frame.

"Can we go inside and talk?" She asks and my mouth goes dry.

"I promise I didn't come here to fight," she assures me so I stiffly nod.

I lead the way to my apartment door and she follows suit, a few steps behind me the entire way until we reach my sitting room.

I gesture at the couch for her to take a seat and she does, unfastening the buckle of her red coat as she sits.

I sit on the arm of the chair opposite, feeling uneasy, nervous and terrified of what's to come.

Lucy is the first one to break the silence.

"You look good Iris," she offers warmly and I give her a polite smile.

"You too Lucy," I reply and it was true.

Her dark hair was sophisticatedly stacked above her head and her subtle make up illuminated her already perfect features. She still had the same quirky smile as she always did many years ago but the maturity in her stance now spoke volumes.

"I don't want to take up too much of your time," Lucy began and I listened intently.

"But I wanted to check in on you and give you something before I leave," she spoke with a resounding confidence that I envied.

"Okay, where you heading?" I asked, curiosity piquing my interest.

"Texas, actually," she beamed and I could tell, the excitement radiated from her.

"You're moving there?" I offered and she smiled.

"Yes, in three weeks. I've been offered a job opportunity that I simply can't refuse. It's a chance for me to own my own restaurant over there," she replied and I could see how proud she was of this fact.

I had to give her due credit, Lucy had always been a hard worker. She'd spent her youth slogging mind-numbing hours and working her way up the chain. We may not have always seen eye-to-eye but I had respect for the woman sat across from me.

"Congratulations Lucy, that's wonderful news," and I meant it.

"Thanks, it's a fresh start you know? A chance to begin again, just the two of us." she spoke this time, her voice quieter and her eyes glistening.

"Me and my daughter Dana," she clarified.

My heart tightened at the name.

Dylan hadn't told me much about his childhood. He had once mentioned an older sister though who had died when he was young. I recalled her name instantaneously as if the conversation had taken place yesterday.

"Of course, I get that," I swallowed hard. "Dana is a beautiful name. How old is your daughter now?" I asked.

"Eight months," Lucy grinned, "I can show you a picture of her if you like?"

My heart ached once more at the prospect.

"Yeah, I'd like that," I nodded and watched as Lucy conjured up the image of the bashful baby girl on her mobile phone.

"Wow, she's just like him," I breathed, my chest feeling tight and my eyes filling up.

"She's Dylan's double for sure," Lucy spoke and at the sound of his name I almost fell apart.

I looked around the room uneasily, unsure of what to say or how to find the words to even begin to try and explain my actions. I'd never imagined in a million years that Lucy Wakefield would be physically sat opposite me in my very own living room. The close proximity of seeing her now had me reeling with regrets. I'd spent weeks and months mulling over how my imagined conversations between us could play out. Right now, my head was an empty space and it was as if I'd been struck dumb.

I cleared my throat and tried to begin;

"Listen, Lucy I am eternally sorry for," but I was cut off.

"Iris, I know. Please, you don't have to say anything. Like I said I came here for two reasons. The first to check in on you. A close friend of mine revealed something about you the other day," she spoke her eyes now focused solely on me.

"Really?" I swallowed again, unsure of what she was implying.

"Yes, at the restaurant. You see my friend had a reservation booked a month ago but called to cancel. She works in the local hospital and told me she'd be unable to make it that evening as she had an emergency to deal with. A woman had been admitted with severe blood loss, after attempting to slice in to her wrists," her eyes never left mine as she spoke.

My blood ran cold at the horrid memory.

"I know it was you Iris. Don't worry my friend never broke her confidentiality agreement. Let's just say I had my suspicions at the time based on her description and I knew back then that there was a possibility it was you. And judging by the colour of your face right now, I think you've confirmed my suspicion was indeed correct." She finished, awaiting my response.

I tugged at the sleeves of my hooded sweatshirt I wore subconsciously trying to hide the scarring that was underneath them. It was as if my soul had been exposed.

"I came here to urge you to seek help Iris. Professional this time. Stop falling in to the pit that will ultimately consume you if you allow it. Learn from the past and move forward. You're no good to the world if you decide to end your own. There's been enough heartache already, for all of us," She spoke soothingly, her eyes filled with an equal measure of sadness and kindness.

My breath hitched in my throat at her sentiment and I fought back my own tears.

"I know how hard it can be to try and move on from tragedy and the difficulty to power through some days, believe me I know. But there is no use in giving up. Lead by example. Prove to others that suicide is *not* an option. We never truly know how our actions impact those around us. You of all people should understand that by now," Lucy's words were hard but they were spoken truthfully.

She was entirely right.

Living with my actions and their consequences was a daily struggle. But it was my struggle to bear. I had to learn to live with that, not try to escape from it. I was responsible for my own fate.

I swiped at the stray tear before making eye contact again.

"You're right, I know that. And I am trying, I've *been* trying, I promise. It's just so hard some days. The guilt, the constant pain," I tried to explain but she held up her hand to silence me so I did, respectfully.

"Don't you think I know that?" She asked, her voice merely a whisper.

"We have that in common Iris. You see, the thing is, you're not the only one having to live with the guilt of a decision they made. A choice that I can no longer ignore. Every day I battle with the same difficulties and guilt that you do.

What if I had stayed instead of fled?

What If I had believed him instead of you?

What if I had listened to Dylan and never read that book?" she posed the questions at me and I shuddered.

"Maybe I could have been the one to stop it you know?

Dylan spent his entire life being there for me since we were kids and just when he really needed me, I bailed on him," Lucy's own tears were falling freely now and I resisted the urge to wipe them away for her.

"I should have seen the signs. I was so hormonal back then and the pregnancy had been my sole focus. I lost sight of the man in front of me and the pain that he was struggling with. I made a wrong choice. It cost him his life," she cried.

I never envisioned that another person shared the same level of heartache and grief as profoundly as I did.

Lucy swiped at her tears with a Kleenex delicately. Even in grief she looked stunning.

"But I have Dana now, and through her I will strive to become better and stronger each and every day.

The world needs strong women. And I want her to grow up knowing that they exist.
And I'll be sure to cherish the memory of her father, each and every day. I will teach Dana when she's old enough to love like he did and tell her stories of all the daft stuff we did as kids. I'll speak fondly of my love for

him and his love for me and the bond we shared because that's what he deserved," Lucy's words were resonating with the deepest part of me.

Her words were inspiring and I admired her courage and strength.

"So promise me you will do the same Iris, no matter what. One day, when you have a child of your own, you'll understand. Until then, you have to keep fighting. It's our duty to remember and honour Dylan for his goodness, not the negative thoughts that troubled him in the end," She finished.

I used my sleeves to dry my eyes once more and took a deep breath in before opening my mouth.

"I will, of course. I owe it to him. It's the least I can do.

 Thank you Lucy, I needed this," I replied hopelessly and then her arms found their way around me.

Our embrace was brief, but it was enough to feel like a huge weight had been lifted. A part of my past had finally been confronted and the power of that shifted something inside me like never before. I still had pain, but the days ahead seemed a little less miserable. My mind cast up the image of the cute little baby girl with the same devilish grin as Dylan and for the first time I felt hope. Hope that the future may not be as bleak as I was led to believe. I only wished Dylan could have been around to see us now.

Lucy stood up then, fastening her coat and composing herself before making her way towards the door.

"Oh, I almost forgot," she spoke before she rustled in to the breast pocket of her red coat and produced a small white envelope.

"This is for you. I don't know exactly what it says, but I have a rough idea. I received one too shortly after we settled the estate."

She clutched at her necklace then, a silver chain with a guitar plectrum attached. My mind quickly assumed it had been gifted to her, once upon a time from Dylan and that whatever he'd written to her had conjured a fond memory.

"Apparently he had instructed his solicitor to give them to us in the event of his passing," she sniffled and I tensed.

So it had been premeditated. I sighed resolutely.

The crisp white envelope had my name scrawled across it in the most familiar handwriting. I held the paper to my chest and thanked Lucy, wishing her safe travels and watching as she departed from my life for good this time.

My hands trembled as I tore the contents from the inside and my mental voice conjured up the sound of Dylan as if he were reading the words aloud.

"Iris,

To the woman who gave up her innocence
In the most precious way
I love you like the summer breeze
In the early midst of May
You came in to my life
In an instant there was a spark
And for that, I'm forever grateful
For the sweet ache you left in my heart

Our ending came as bittersweet
But I'm no longer mad at you
Your actions came from heartache
That much was true.

So live on as you were meant to,
Beautiful and adoring
For Iris Steadman, to me you were an enigma,
Enchanting and alluring.

Love always, D x"

I traced my fingertips over the cursive and kissed the ink before folding up the precious note and placing it inside my jewellery box above the mantelpiece.

Snuggled on the single seater in my sitting room, I wept for hours.

I cried until my mind finally found the reprieve from the years of sorrow I'd endured at the hands of my own foolish vendetta.

I cried with relief in knowing that at one time, Dylan had loved me. That we had shared some special moments and that I could now move on with my life knowing that he still had it in his heart to forgive me for my behaviour in the end.

I cried for the little girl who would grow up without a father and then I cried some more for the woman who moments earlier, shared the same harrowing guilt that I did.

I cried until I knew for certain my tears were spent.

I splashed my face down with cool water from the sink before returning to my bedroom.

Grabbing my docking station from the nightstand and my old iPod from the desk drawer, I lay back on my bed.

And then, for the first time in years, I let the sound of Dylan's song voice fill the empty room.

I closed my eyes, smiling to myself and allowed the music to consume me.

Acknowledgements

To my husband for your never ending support, words of encouragement and endearing qualities. Some of which drive me crackers and others that catapult me to become better with every passing year.

To my son and daughter. Becoming a mother has transformed me to become even more compassionate and empathetic and I try to use those traits with every character I create. Your unconditional love is the greatest attribute a person could wish for.

To Kenneth Watt, my fellow artist and companion when it comes to writing and general matters of the heart. Your friendship has pulled me through all kinds of like affirming moments through the years. Here's to growing old.

To Jamie Mathers for allowing me to use that gorgeously haunting image of you on the front cover and to all the lads in Dude Trips who continue to produce catchy and heartfelt songs that remind me of what it's like growing up where we come from. You're making us all proud boys.

To Chris Sherrit, my fellow author friend. Thank you for your critique, editing skills and honesty. Here's to future releases.

A special shout out to my fellow mamma and all round life-saving agony aunt Stacy Adams for keeping me sane in times of distress and reminding me that it's ok to let the household chores slide every once in a while. Have a glass (or two!) of wine on me babe!

Finally, a respectful shout out to all of you lovely readers, the men and women who fight battles with themselves in order to get through the day. Life is horrendously tough sometimes but the human mind is stronger than you can ever imagine. Speak up, speak out and don't ever be ashamed to be yourself. Above all, spread love. Be there and show you care.

If you or anyone you know is struggling and in need of help, please do not hesitate to reach out. Contact the Suicide Prevention line by visiting their website:

www.suicide-prevention.org.uk

If you live outside the UK, please contact your local support services.

Printed in Great Britain
by Amazon

85808542R00099